BROKEN TOGETHER

… 'For this reason, a man shall leave his father and mother and shall be joined inseparably to his wife, and the two shall become one flesh',
Matthew 19:5 AMP

Taiwo Iredele Odubiyi

PRAISES FOR THE BOOKS OF TAIWO IREDELE ODUBIYI

If I had come across your books earlier, I might have escaped this horrible marriage I'm presently into (I'm a pastor's wife!) 😭 😭 Now that I have known about your books since a few years ago, and have read almost all of them except the newly released, I'm buying them for my daughters as well (in fact, they have fallen in love with your books). I believe that with God, and with the inspirations that your books carry, my daughters will not make a mistake. 🔖 Thank you for allowing God to use you Ma – *a reader*

You are a prolific writer. I do not flatter. It is not in my DNA. *"She who has a man."* I just never thought of such a story line. Looking forward to getting to read *"Never Say Never."* – *Lenient Bilewu (Mrs.) USA*

The practicality of your writings is what makes them so endearing and widely accepted and read. On this latest piece, kudos, first to your Enabler- God, and second, to you- for continuing to be a channel of blessing through your unmissable writings ✍. My perspective on Comfort & Joy: A Christian (fiancé) with his inner caution activated and outward action equally guarded was yet found appraising a woman when he was let into some hitherto undisclosed information about her. For people with great character, even the vicissitudes of life cannot permanently keep them at the backside of life! It's the reason an ill-mannered single girl would still lose her advantage to a widowed but well-mannered woman whose intrinsic goodness flows naturally to any potential suitor- including someone's fiancé! That is life... that a faithful and committed fiancé could not resist recognizing superior quality in a widow whose lowly background made her evidently unqualified to pose any threat to his fiancée...but there is an old saying that "character is everything!" Here's another sterling piece from the stable of our prolific writer who needs no introduction. Her *"Comfort & Joy"* is a novel you must read and finish at a go...because it's both concise and absolutely alluring! - ***Babatope Olabode, Lagos, Nigeria***

I am sooooooo happy to finally meet you. I started reading your books in 2004/2005. I had almost all the series *SHADOWS FROM THE PAST, IN LOVE FOR US, LOVE FEVER, LOVE ON THE PULPIT, THIS TIME AROUND, TO LOVE AGAIN, OH BABY, TEARS ON MY PILLOW*, etc. Whaooooooooo. My siblings lent our neighbors and I lost the books. Fortunately for me, I received a minister's voucher from my church on Tuesday. I went to Bible Wonderland and then I saw your book! 😹😹😹😹😹😹😹. I was so happy I packed all the titles on the shelf. 😄😄😄😄😄 I packed so teyyy I took Igbo book join 🤣🤣🤣🤣🤣 I can't read it. I'll have to give it to one of my Igbo friends that can read it. I couldn't take all that I packed because I'd exceeded my voucher pay 😩😩😩 but I got some. I am going back to get those ones I left. My sister is about to hijack the ones I bought sef😳 😔. Thanks for blessing lives – *Oluwakemi Senami Oni, Lagos, Nigeria*

Highlight of my day. Hi family. I said I was going to gift myself Taiwo Iredele Odubiyi's books as Christmas gifts and here we are! I was only able to get 7, as in … I'm so happy! I started reading her books when I was in secondary school. I started with *Tears on my pillow* and I am sooo into them. There was a time I just couldn't get her books anymore but now I got in touch with her again and here we are. Guys, please gift yourself something for Christmas. And I'm sure buying her books.... you won't regret it – *Anu Asaoye, Nigeria*

Thanks for yielding to God. Your books have always been a source of blessing to me for over 13 years now – *Allen Oluwaseun, Abeokuta, Nigeria*

Your books are so inspiring. God bless you, Ma. Thank you for allowing yourself to be used by God. You are indeed a blessing to this generation. I hope to keep all your books for my children to read too – *Funmilayo Ogundipe, Ile Ife, Nigeria*

I have the hardcopy of *Is it me you're looking for*, and I have read it over and over. Love your books. I have learnt a lot of lessons and with the help of God, I have been teaching others – *Oluwabusayo Adebisi, Tede, Oyo state, Nigeria*

Comfort and Joy, I got mine already on okadabooks. As usual, I enjoyed this again. Such a blessing to me. Thanks for availing yourself for the Master's use. I have indeed been blessed – *Mrs. Eunice Adegoke, lecturer, Kaduna state, Nigeria*

If you could see me now – so sweet. This is a message on its own. This is purely God's word in a story – ***Smiletickles***

Going through the pages of this great book *IS IT ME YOU'RE LOOKING FOR?*, I can't help but picture myself in the same situation as Jite where she is trusting God for the right man. I believe God will guard me to the right person too. Thank you for allowing God to use you through writing in reaching out to us. God bless your ministry greatly. I love you – ***Ukahi Gift, Sagamu, Nigeria***

Love on the Pulpit... Intriguing. Keep publishing! – *Jegede **Eniola***

I just love everything about this book – *In Love For Us*. If Ben had not been successful, Tolu would have been thanking her mother for separating them, but reverse is the case – ***Oluwatunmise Rachael***

Never Say Never – Spectacular! – ***Onaopemiposi Bamidele***

EXCERPTS

... She frowned and stared at him. That was not what he was supposed to say. "Are you trying to push me away, Chris?!"

He wanted to say ... *no, I'm not. I'm only trying to make you know that you can leave.* But he changed his mind, returned the stare and said, "Maybe I am."

Surprised, she paused as if to absorb this, and then she retorted, "Oh, really? Why, if I may ask?" ...

... She also counselled them on how to handle sexual intimacy. She told Stella, "Let him know what you need him to do." And looking at Chris, she said, "Tell your wife what you like." ...

... Chris saw her face break into a beautiful smile, and that made him happy. He loved to see her smile ...

ACKNOWLEDGMENTS

I thank You, Lord God, the I AM, my Rescuer and Lord,
For:

Yet another book. *Thank You for the great privilege and grace that You have given me to speak and write for You, and about You: about Your will, Your ways, Your word, and Your wondrous love. Thank You for the mercy You have shown me to know You;*

All the wonderful family members that You have blessed me with – *for all that they do, and always being there for me.*

The editor of this book—TanitOluwa Odubiyi. *Thank you for choosing to work with me. I appreciate you.*

Friends, fans, and my avid readers - those who have been with me since the beginning of this great journey, and those who joined along the way, reading my books, supporting, praying, and encouraging me.

Lord, let those who read this book be blessed, touched and transformed by You, that they may know that You are the real Author and Your mercy truly endures forever!

It's All About You!   Taiwo Iredele Odubiyi

DEDICATION

To God

&

To all the people out there with physical challenges, especially those whose lives were altered as a result of an accident. This is to encourage you and make you know that you can still enjoy life and fulfil your divine purpose.

My brethren, count it all joy when you fall into various trials, knowing that the testing of your faith produces patience. But let patience have its perfect work, that you may be perfect and complete, lacking nothing. If any of you lacks wisdom, let him ask of God, Who gives to all liberally and without reproach, and it will be given to him. Blessed is the man who endures temptation; for when he has been approved, he will receive the crown of life which the Lord has promised to those who love Him.

James 1:2-5, 12 NKJV

 CHAPTER 1

STELLA, WHO SAT beside her husband, Chris, smiled broadly as she looked at John and her cousin, Lola, as they exchanged their marriage vows.

The day was Saturday, the fifth of December, and the time now was ten-fifty in the morning. John and Lola were being joined in holy matrimony at *Word of God Church*, the church where Lola worshipped and where she was an ordained pastor. The church hall, which had been transformed with drapes and balloons of different colors for the wedding, was filled to full capacity with families, friends, and well-wishers who had come to rejoice with the new couple and their parents.

Lola's mother, Seun Alabi, was one of the biggest female actresses in the country, and several movie producers and movie stars had turned up to support and rejoice with one of their own. A host of press and photographers were also in attendance.

Soon, the senior pastor of the church who was conducting the solemnization announced, "As John and Lola have given themselves to each other by the promises they have exchanged, I now pronounce them husband and wife, in the name of the Father, and of the Son, and of the Holy Spirit."

The congregation said *Amen*.

The pastor went on. "Let everyone everywhere recognize and respect this holy union now and forever."

The congregation said *Amen* again.

"You may now kiss your bride." The pastor told John, and amidst cheers, John turned to Lola for their very first kiss.

As Stella looked on, the ceremony reminded her of her own wedding. This was her and Chris on the twenty-fifth of April.

Even though the wedding was seven months ago, it still seemed like yesterday to her, and she and Chris still felt like a newlywed couple. She was now twenty seven years old while he was thirty years.

Stella and Chris met in university when she was in her first year studying accounting while he was two years ahead of her studying electrical engineering. At the time, Chris who was tall and dark in complexion, was twenty one years old. He seemed to be the perfect man for eighteen-year-old Stella who was also tall, slim, and dark in complexion like her father.

They liked each other and started a relationship, but before the year ended, she gave her life to Jesus and became a Christian. As her walk with God deepened, she realized that the relationship with Chris was ungodly, and she ended it as difficult as it was for her to do. Some weeks later, she saw him on campus with another lady. It hadn't taken him long to move on, apparently. Knowing that she was the one who ended their relationship, she did not allow herself to feel bad, and she focused on her education and spiritual growth. The following year, Chris graduated from the university and she felt relieved that she would no longer run into him and his girlfriend on campus.

In her third year at the university, she liked a man in the campus fellowship that she attended and began to pray for God's will to be done. Only to discover that the man was already taken! After her graduation and NYSC, which was a mandatory national service by Nigerian university graduates, she got a job in an auditing firm at the age of twenty three, and where she still worked.

One day, she and a senior colleague went to a manufacturing company on an official assignment only to run into Chris there. He told her that he worked for the company as an engineer. They exchanged pleasantries and phone numbers, and he promised to call her later. He did, and while talking, he revealed that he had also become a Christian and now worshipped at *Living Word Evangelical Church.*

They kept in touch and soon began to pray about marriage when they realized that they still cared about each other. With time, they informed their parents and pastors and got their approval. Shortly after, Chris left the manufacturing company for a better-paying job at *Powerhouse Electric Company.* Stella was happy for him and told him that she also had plans to leave the auditing firm within the next two years.

On their wedding day, Stella felt on top of the world. She was driven to the church where she and Chris would be joined in holy matrimony in a well-decorated Mercedes-Benz car, with her father and maid of honor seated beside her, and her mother in the front passenger seat.

Stella looked every inch a happy and beautiful bride in her white wedding dress—and indeed, she had every reason to be happy. She was a Christian, had a good job, and now had a tall and handsome husband who was not only a Christian but also had a good job. On the wedding day, Chris wore a black wedding suit that looked good on him. The framed photos in the living room of their apartment were a constant reminder of the joy that filled their hearts on their wedding day.

Before the wedding, Stella and Chris had agreed to wait a year after the wedding before starting a family. They still stood by the agreement, and that was why she had not yet conceived and her tummy remained flat. They would like to enjoy themselves before becoming parents and having the responsibilities of taking care of little children. When they would start having children, they might need to have someone live with them to support them; but, for now, they would like to be alone. This 'alone' period would also help them to bond and learn more about each other.

They loved each other, and Stella thanked God daily for blessing her with Chris. He was active, hardworking, and very intelligent.

While Stella was still looking at the new couple—John and Lola—and remembering her own wedding, Chris suddenly laughed. She looked at him and saw him focused on the new couple.

Still smiling, she nudged him and asked, "Doesn't this remind you of our own wedding?"

Chris nodded, and reaching out to take her hand, he gave it a gentle squeeze and held on to it.

Stella looked away from her husband and rested her gaze on another cousin, Mercy, who sat on her other side. Mercy was also smiling as she used her phone to take pictures of the new couple. Mercy, who was a year younger than Stella, got married two months ago, and her husband, Dayo, was one of John's groomsmen. Mercy and Stella were not just cousins; they were also friends.

One of Mercy's closest female friends, Lekan, and Lekan's fiancé, Victor, were on Mercy's other side. When Stella first met the lady, Lekan, she had been surprised at her name because she thought it was a male's name. When she commented on it, Lekan laughed. She said people told her that all the time, however if one considered the meaning of the full name, it shouldn't be limited to only males. Olamilekan means *my wealth or blessing has increased by one.*

Stella returned her gaze to where the pastor stood with John and Lola.

The pastor introduced the new couple to the congregation, and beaming with joy, the new couple waved their hands at the people.

As Stella smiled back at Lola and John, she could still remember how the couple met, and she cast her mind to the past— about a year ago—precisely on the first day of January. Dayo, who was now Mercy's husband, had organized a get-together for his friends in his apartment on January 1st to celebrate the New Year. Since Dayo and his friends were committed Christians, Mercy had decided to invite her very good friend, Lekan, to the get-together so that she could be introduced to one of Dayo's unmarried friends, John. Mercy had also invited her older cousin, Lola, to the event with the hope that Lola would encounter one of Dayo's other male friends and that they would be interested in getting to know each other better. But as it turned out at the event, before Lekan could be introduced to John, John encountered Lola in the kitchen and exchanged information with her.

Lekan had felt embarrassed and a little upset at the turn of events, but as God would have it, she was now engaged to the man who sat beside her at the get-together—Victor. They would be getting married next year.

Lola had not thought much about her encounter with John in Dayo's kitchen. She had not even wanted to attend the event, but now she and John had just been pronounced husband and wife. Stella couldn't help thinking that God was indeed good.

Stella brought her mind back to the present, and as she glanced around, her eyes settled on Lola's mother, who was one of her aunts. A couple was beside Lola's mother, and next to the couple was Lola's father, a professor. He was not married to Lola's mother, Seun Alabi. (**Author's note:** *Accidentally Yours).*

On Seun Alabi's other side were Stella's grandparents, whom all the family members called Grandpa and Grandma. Still glancing around, Stella saw her parents and her father's sisters where they sat.

Chris' parents and older brother, Emmanuel, popularly called Emman, were also present. Emman was five years older than Chris and married with children. Even though he had a university degree, he was a car dealer. He started the business three years ago, and had an office with two employees. Chris' younger brother, Luke, lived in Canada.

Before returning her gaze to the activity going on in front of the altar inside the hall, Stella also saw some movie stars whom she recognized.

The introduction of John and Lola as the latest couple in town was followed by the church choir's ministration, before John's pastor, Dave, was invited to give the word of exhortation. In his brief message, Pastor Dave admonished married couples never to leave God out of their affairs and to remain committed to each other. At the end, he made an altar call, and among the people who came out to give their lives to Jesus were some of the movie stars.

When the service eventually ended, Stella and her husband joined their families and friends outside of the hall to take pictures with the new couple.

Afterward, they walked up to Stella's parents, where they stood talking with a man. They had brought Stella's parents to the church, and they were supposed to go to the reception venue together.

Stella greeted the man standing with her parents and then informed her father, "Papa, we are ready to leave."

"You can leave. We will go with my friend." Her father said and pointed at the man beside him.

Stella's father, Mr. Alabi, was nicknamed Papa by his nieces and nephews because he played the role of a big brother to his four younger sisters. And now, even his children usually called him Papa.

He was the first of Grandpa and Grandma's five children and the only male. Mercy's mother was his immediate younger sister, followed by Lola's mother—Seun Alabi—and then two younger sisters. When Mercy's mother died eleven years ago, Papa brought Mercy and her siblings into his house and took care of them along with his own five children. Mercy lived with the family until she got married in October, while her two younger siblings still lived with Mr. Alabi's family.

Hand in hand, Chris and Stella left the church hall and headed for Chris' black SUV, where it was parked.

On the way to the reception hall, with Chris behind the wheel, they continued talking.

"I almost can't believe that our own wedding was seven months ago." Stella commented. "How time flies! Wow!"

Chris smiled. "Hmm mmm."

"And some of the people in my bridal party are now married, while some are engaged to be married." Stella added.

As she began to mention the names of the ladies in her bridal party, she mentioned Mercy and her friend, Lekan, and she recalled that Victor proposed to Lekan at her reception venue's parking lot.

Chris and Stella continued talking, and soon they reached the reception venue and alighted from the car. At the hall entrance, they were welcomed by an usher. Inside the hall, they spotted their parents and Chris' brother where they sat, and as they made their way to the table, they noted that the hall was beautiful.

The event went well, and when it ended around five in the evening, Stella's parents followed Stella and Chris to their SUV.

Stella's mother, Mrs. Alabi, was in the ice-block-making business, while Stella's father, a retired police officer, had a shop where building materials were sold.

Mr. and Mrs. Alabi's first child, a female, was married and lived in Jos with her husband. Stella, an accountant, was the second child. The remaining three children were males. The first and second sons were architects, while the youngest son was an undergraduate at a university.

On the way to her parents' house to drop them off, Stella asked her mother if she would be able to make puff-puff soon as she would like to have some. Puff-puff, which was made of fried dough was one of Stella's favorite African snacks.

"I made it yesterday. You can have some." Her mother said.

"Good."

When they reached the gray-painted house owned by her parents, Stella asked Chris to give her some minutes. She got down and followed her parents, while Chris stayed in the car to make a call and respond to some texts and e-mails. About fifteen minutes later, she returned to the car with a bag in her hand.

As Chris pulled back on the road, Stella brought out a covered bowl from the bag and prayed over it.

"Would you want one?" She asked Chris.

In response, he stretched a hand to her, and she chuckled. Taking one, she put it in his hand and took one for herself.

The drive to their house took about forty five minutes, and when they arrived, the house's employed gateman opened the black gate of the house as Chris drove inside. The beautiful house had two apartments on the ground floor and another two on the upper floor. Chris and Stella occupied the apartment at the back of the upper floor.

When they reached their three-bedroom rented apartment, Chris brought out a key, unlocked the front door, and they stepped inside the tastefully furnished living room. It was very neat, with no sock, shoe, paper, or cloth lying around.

Both of them liked Christmas, and they had decorated the room together for Christmas just yesterday. This was their first Christmas together as a married couple, and Stella had made plans for how they would spend the Christmas holiday.

Stella walked over to the Christmas tree that was in a corner, plugged in the lights on the tree, and the lights began to twinkle in a beautiful way.

Chris sat on the nearest seat. "I need to make a call." He said and began to remove his shoes and socks.

"Please don't leave your shoes and socks there." She told him as she went toward their bedroom.

"I won't."

"That was what you said last night when we returned from Lola and John's traditional engagement ceremony, but you did. I had to put them away this morning when I was cleaning up. The same thing happened twice last week."

"I apologize, but I've told you not to bother yourself about my stuff. I will put them away eventually."

"You know how I feel about that. I like things to be organized." She said.

Yes, he knew that. People who knew Stella well knew that she liked being organized, and she was always quick to say that everything had a place. Being organized helped her feel in control of situations around her.

Chris changed his mind. He got up, took his phone, shoes, and socks, and followed Stella into their bedroom.

The large room with white painted walls and a gray rug was clean and pretty. Their queen-size bed had a beautiful headboard, and on the two sides of the bed were small tables with three drawers to keep away loose things. On each table was a small lamp for late-night reading. The bed, which was covered with a white sheet, had a large white blanket and five accent pillows. And on the wall by the bed was a black script, '*Together Forever,*' which made a nice contrast to the white wall. On the other side of the wall was their framed wedding photograph. The room with a large closet also had a dresser, an oval-shaped mirror by the dresser, a chair, a white ceiling fan, and a flat-screen TV on a wall.

Putting his stuff away, Chris sat on the chair in the room to make his call. It didn't take long, and soon both of them had showered and worn casuals.

Deciding to stay in their bedroom, they stacked their pillows against the bed headboard and relaxed against them. As they watched a documentary on TV and talked, they ate some of the puff-puff balls from Stella's mother. A tray was between them on the bed, and on it were the TV remote, two small bottles of juice, and a bowl that contained puff-puff.

Stella had had a manicure and pedicure on Thursday, and now she looked at her hands, admiring how fresh they looked. *Lie was good,* she thought. *Really, really good.* She had about everything she could possibly need in life: a wonderful husband; a loving family; reliable friends; a good job; and a relationship with God.

At about eight that evening, Chris received a call from one of his close friends. The friend was in the neighborhood and wanted to know if Chris was at home. Chris said yes, and within fifteen minutes, the friend showed up with his fiancé. They didn't stay long, and afterward, Chris and Stella had dinner and returned to their bedroom. They eventually prayed and prepared to sleep.

In the church they attended, *Living Word Evangelical Church,* Stella was a chorister and Chris was one of the Sunday morning Bible study teachers. Like Stella, Chris was a good singer, but he wasn't in the choir. Being church workers, they had to be in church thirty minutes before the Sunday morning Bible study would start at nine-thirty so they could pray with the other workers and prepare for the church service.

Chris and Stella woke up at seven-thirty in the morning of the next day, and as it would take about twenty-eight minutes to drive to church, they left the house about an hour later. In church, the Bible study started and ended at the right time, and the main service began promptly at ten. When it ended around one in the afternoon, Stella and Chris left the church almost immediately, as they would still be coming back at six in the evening for couples' fellowship, which held the first Sunday of each month.

 CHAPTER 2

ON THE WAY home, Chris and Stella stopped at a restaurant to buy food, which they ate when they got home. Afterward, they laid down in bed together, talking and relaxing for some time. At four-thirty, they got up to prepare for church.

When they arrived at church at six-fifteen, they found thirteen couples in the church's event hall, including the pastor and his wife. The praise and worship session had started, and they joined the service.

The session was followed by a number of activities, and when it was time for exhortation, the pastor's wife stood with her Bible and iPad and went to the front of the hall, where there was a pulpit.

She prayed briefly and then announced that she was going to talk about intimacy in marriage. After introducing the topic, she asked them to open their Bibles to Song of Solomon, chapter two and verse six. She opened hers and read the verse.

His left hand is under my head, and his right hand embraces me.

She explained the scripture and encouraged married couples to sleep this way, with the husband's hand under his wife's head while the second hand embraces her.

As she talked about the importance of intimacy in marriage, everyone laughed, including her husband, the senior pastor. They were obviously enjoying the discussion.

Chris and Stella also found it interesting, and they were learning some things that would help their young marriage. Most of the time, after sexual intimacy and prayer, Chris turned to his side of the bed and took a book to read, while Stella would put her hand on his shoulder or waist and then prepare to sleep. But as they listened to the pastor's wife now, they planned to put the teaching into practice and change some things. Stella would put her head on Chris' shoulder, and Chris would no longer turn his back to Stella in bed, starting that night.

The service lasted two hours, and after refreshments were served, they dispersed.

At home, Chris and Stella had dinner, and in bed with each person's head on a pillow, facing up, Chris shared the Word of God briefly. When he was through, he asked Stella to pray. She did, and he said Amen.

When Stella was ready to sleep, Chris put his left hand down. She snuggled close, rested her head in the hollow, and he embraced her with his other hand.

"Hmm, I love this." She whispered.

He smiled and kissed the top of her head.

After about ten minutes, he removed the hand that embraced her, took from his bedside table the book he had started reading the previous day, and with his second hand still under her head, he began to read.

Soon, he could hear Stella snoring gently. He eased his arm away from under her head, adjusted himself to be more comfortable, and continued reading the book. He read for about an hour, after which he put the book down and turned the overhead light off. He turned back to face his wife, put a hand by her waist, and soon slept off.

Stella usually woke up before her husband in the morning of a weekday at five so she could prepare breakfast for them both. And that Monday morning, she made two pieces of toast bread and hot chocolate tea for Chris and packed them up in his insulated food bag.

Chris woke up shortly after, and by seven, he was ready to leave the house. They kissed and said goodbye, and he left, carrying his food bag.

Some minutes later, she also left the house in her car, a light blue Toyota Corolla, and headed to work. Her insulated food bag was on the front passenger seat.

****

As Chris drove toward the office, he thought of the meetings he had lined up for the day. The company he worked for— Powerhouse Electric Company—had some building projects at hand that included the installation of electrical systems in a university complex that was being built by someone. This particular project had been assigned to him, and he would have to meet the client at ten this morning to discuss the project. Afterward, he would go to the project site. At four in the afternoon, he would need to return to the office to see his boss to assess the progress on the project so that necessary changes could be implemented.

Seeing that it would be a busy day for him, he decided to have his breakfast now. When he stopped at a traffic light, he opened his food box that was on the front passenger seat, brought out the foil-wrapped two pieces of toast bread, and put them on the seat beside the box. He removed his small tea bottle from the box and put it in one of the cup holders by his seat.

The light changed to green, and as he drove on with his left hand firmly on the wheel, he took a toast bread with his second hand.

He had just taken a bite when his phone, which was in his shirt pocket, began to ring. He put the bread down and grabbed his phone. The call was from one of the draftsmen regarding the university project, and he answered it. The call lasted about three minutes, and he returned the phone to his pocket. He would need to contact an architect to inform him of his discussion with the draftsman, but knowing that the architect would not be available at this time, he decided to send a text to him.

Taking the bread again, he began to eat. When he finished eating it, he carried the tea bottle and sipped a little.

He put the bottle in the cup holder, and as he wanted to bring out his phone to send a text, he sensed in his spirit that he should not drive and text. The text could wait until he got to the office.

He stopped and considered this counsel. *Hmm, maybe I should wait.*

But another voice told him to go ahead. He could text and drive; after all, he was a good and careful driver. He got his driver's license at the age of eighteen and had never been involved in an accident. Besides, people drive and text all the time. He had done it before, and he could do it again, the voice told him.

Chris decided to go with the second voice. It would be a short text that would not take more than about a minute. And he would be careful, he told himself.

Bringing out the phone, he opened contacts and began to type the person's name so he could search for it.

He typed four letters and looked up, only to see a bus coming straight at him from the side.

"Jesus!" Chris shouted.

But before he could swerve to avoid it, the bus hit his vehicle with force. His SUV spun around and landed on the other side of the road, where an oncoming vehicle rammed it. This impact made his car hit some other cars and eventually got pinned between them.

Chris was immediately covered in blood. Knowing he had been severely injured, he tried to move and get out of the car so he could be helped, but he could not. Scared, he took a deep breath and tried again, but couldn't move.

He could hear the shouts of people. Then he seemed to hear someone yell, "Help!" but he wasn't sure if that was him or another person as things suddenly became hazy. The last he heard was his scream of "Jesus!", and then all at once everything went black. He did not see as some drivers got out of their cars and rushed toward his car to help him. Some passersby went after the driver of the bus, pulled him out of the vehicle, and began to beat him, blaming him for the accident.

****

Stella worked at *Abiola Davids & co.*, a consulting firm that provided accounting and auditing services to clients.

She reached the office at eight-ten, drove inside the compound and parked her car. She saw the man who had been contracted to decorate the office reception for Christmas; he was standing in front of the four storey building, talking with some men. She alighted from her car with her handbag and food bag, and when she reached the men, she greeted them. The consulting firm occupied the entire ground floor and she walked toward the front entrance of the building.

Inside, she greeted the receptionist at the front desk and as she walked down the hallway with offices on each side, her shoes made clicking sounds on the marble floor. She soon reached the office she shared with two of her colleagues, Ade and Bimbo. They had arrived and she greeted them.

As she exchanged pleasantries with them, she walked over to her table and put the bags in her hand on it. On the black table were neatly stacked files, a pen holder, and a small photo frame of her and Chris. On the floor beside the table was a small trash bin and under the table was a pair of black slippers that she wore in the office for comfort. The back of her black leather chair was draped with a black jacket which she kept there to wear whenever the office got too cold for comfort.

Today would be busy as usual. She would be going to a client's warehouse this morning for stocktaking which would take the whole day.

She was about to sit down and pray briefly as she usually did when her phone began to ring inside her handbag. She opened her handbag, brought out her phone, and checked. It was her husband.

"Honey," she said cheerily.

"Hello?"

It was a man's voice but not Chris'.

Wondering who it was, she spoke again, "Hello?"

"Hello? Can you hear me?" The unfamiliar male voice asked.

"Yes. Who is this please?" She demanded and frowned slightly, sounding puzzled. Why was Chris' phone with this man?

"Are you the wife of the owner of this phone?"

What?! "Yes. Who are you?" She asked sharply, wondering who was on the line and what he wanted. And more importantly, where was Chris? She hoped Chris had not been abducted and this was a call for ransom. *God, don't let it be!*

She added, "Where's the owner of the phone? Where's my husband?"

Hearing her questions and the concern in her voice, her colleagues were now staring at her, wondering what the call was about.

The caller responded, "I'm sorry to call you, but the owner of the phone was involved in a serious car accident and -"

"A car accident?!" Stella repeated as she suddenly began to tremble all over. *Chris*! "Where? What happened? Can I talk to my husband?" She requested.

Her colleagues left their seats and came to her, looking concerned.

"You can't talk to him now. I am one of the people who witnessed the accident and rushed over to help the victims." The caller told her.

Victims?! She could hardly breath now. Was Chris dead?!

The man was still talking and he identified himself as a paediatrician. "I assisted in getting the victims to the hospital nearest to the scene of the accident."

"Jesus!"

Her colleagues asked her, "What's that? What happened?"

"The person is saying that my husband was involved in an accident! He said he's one of the people who witnessed the accident and assisted in getting the victims to a hospital." Stella explained with trembling voice.

"Is he telling you the truth?" Bimbo, a female, asked.

"Let me talk to the person." Ade said and held out his hand to take the phone.

Stella gave it to him.

"Calm down, Stella." Bimbo said.

"Hello, who is this please?" Ade spoke into the phone, and put it on speaker so others could hear the person on the line.

"I'm Dr. Abel Kanu, a paediatrician." The stranger said and repeated what he told Stella.

Ade asked some questions and got more details about the accident.

"So, which hospital is the owner of this phone in? Kindly give me the name and address of the hospital please."

When Stella heard that, she quickly opened her handbag and brought out pen and paper to write the information.

Abel dictated the information, and spoke again, "The hospital would like to know the names of the owner of this phone for identification."

The colleague looked at Stella for approval as he said, "Chris Brume."

Stella nodded.

"Alright." Abel responded.

"So, how is Chris, er ... the owner of this phone? How serious is this?" Ade asked.

"He's not dead if that's what you're trying to know." Abel answered.

"Is he going to be alright?"

Abel hesitated a little before he said, "Well, I wouldn't know. I'm just one of those who assisted the people involved. But apparently, the bus driver who caused the accident was drunk and he smashed into Chris' car. I guess that Chris should have seen the driver but he didn't. Some policemen have been called and they will be able to give you more information later."

Stella became greatly troubled when she heard that. Was Chris dead and the man just did not want to say so?—she wondered, thinking the worst.

Abel went on to explain that he found Chris' phone on the floor of the driver's seat, and that it was a good thing that his phone was not locked.

"If it was locked, I wouldn't have been able to get his wife's contact."

"That's true." Ade agreed.

"And it's a good thing that it was not found by a wrong person. That would have caused more problems." Abel added.

"How will I get Chris' phone?" Stella whispered to Ade in the background.

Ade asked the man the question and he said he would give the phone to Mariam, one of the nurses attending to Chris.

# CHAPTER 3

ADE THANKED ABEL and said that Stella would go to the hospital right away.

While Ade was still talking to Abel, Stella began to remove her shoes so she could wear the black slippers under her table. Putting the shoes under the table, she carried her handbag, ready to leave the office. She didn't care about her food bag now.

Immediately the call ended, she informed her colleagues that she would have to see her boss to take permission so she could be on her way, and her colleagues followed her. As they left their office, she prayed for divine intervention for Chris, and the others said Amen.

"He will be fine." Ade told her.

In the boss' office, Stella couldn't talk as tears filled her eyes, and she struggled to control her emotions.

"What happened?" Her boss asked, concerned.

"She received a call just now." Ade answered and then explained about the phone call.

"Oh, I'm sorry to hear that." The elderly man said, deeply sympathetic. "Of course, you will need to go and see your husband."

Stella nodded.

"And I don't think that you should go alone since you're not sure about the call. Someone should go with you. What if it's a setup—a trap of some sort?" The man pointed out.

Ade nodded in agreement and volunteered to go with Stella.

"With the way she's feeling, trembling all over, I think that you should drive." The boss told Ade.

"Yes sir." Ade agreed.

The boss stood and looked at Stella. "Er ... what were you supposed to do this morning?"

That was when Stella remembered that she was supposed to be at the warehouse by eleven. She explained to her boss, and he asked her to handover to Bimbo.

Grateful for her boss' thoughtfulness, she thanked him.

As Stella and her colleagues walked back to their office, Ade suggested that it would be better to go in his car, and Stella agreed. In the office, while she quickly explained the work to be done at the warehouse and gave necessary documents to Bimbo, Ade cleared his table and took his car key.

"I'm ready." He told Stella and shortly after, they left the office.

Stella had planned to visit someone in the evening on her way home, but, that would no longer be possible if indeed her husband was involved in an accident.

As they walked out of the building toward Ade's car, Stella's mind raced about what to do next, who to call. But what if the news was not true?

They reached the car and entered it, with Stella in the front passenger seat and Ade behind the wheel.

"Your husband will be alright." Ade told her reassuringly as he started the car.

As soon as the car left the compound, Stella called the phone of the senior pastor of the church that she and Chris attended, but it was picked by the pastor's personal assistant. The PA explained that the pastor and his wife were at a program. The pastor would be ministering soon and might not be able to receive calls now. However, but when Stella explained the reason for the call, the PA said that he would give the phone to the pastor and asked her to hold on. When the senior pastor came on the line, he wanted to know what happened and Stella briefly explained. He prayed for Chris and asked Stella to call his wife's phone whenever she got to the hospital, so that they could know the situation of things. He also said that one or two of his pastors would come to the hospital.

When the call ended, Stella put the phone down, and stared out the window. However, she wasn't seeing any of the passing scenery as she thought of different things.

Could the call be some form of prank? Was today the first day of April, and someone was playing an April fool's joke on her? She thought about today's date, and told herself – *No. Today's the seventh of December, not the first of April.* Besides, she and Chris did not do such silly things. They had never done it.

Could Chris be in his office? Could it be that his phone was stolen by the person who called? She thought about it and felt that what the caller said was true; but still, she decided to call Chris' office.

She glanced at the time on the dashboard. It was now nine-twenty. Taking her phone, she dialled his boss' line. "Hello?"

When the man said that no one had seen Chris, Stella knew then that the bad news was true. Chris would have been in the office by now if there was no problem.

She told the man about the call she received, and shocked, he said that a staff member would come over to the hospital.

"Don't hesitate to let me know if there's anything I can do to help." Chris' boss added.

Stella called Chris' phone to see if Nurse Mariam would pick it or better still, Chris himself, to assure her that he was fine. She half-hoped to hear his voice, but the call didn't go through. The phone had been switched off. Yes, something had happened to her husband. There was no more doubt in her mind.

Ade spoke, "It would be necessary to know where his car is and get it towed."

"That's true. Oh my God!" She exclaimed. That had not occurred to her.

"Someone will need to visit the accident scene." Ade added.

"Yes. Do you have that man's phone number—Dr. Abel?"

"No, I didn't remember to ask him for it. Do you need it?"

"Yes, in case we need more information about the accident." She said.

She had never been involved in a serious accident. So she didn't know if the accident would have to be reported to the police first or the insurance company or if the car should be towed away from the accident spot first. When she was learning to drive, she had hit a car, but it wasn't serious.

She called Chris' brother, Emman, to inform him.

"I'm on my way to the hospital." She added. "I don't think that you need to tell Daddy and Mommy yet since it has not been confirmed."

"No, not now." Emman agreed. "I will leave my office as soon as I can and come over. Please forward the name and address of the hospital to me."

"I will." She promised. "Another thing ... I don't know where his vehicle is. Someone will need to visit the accident scene immediately. Can you handle it for me please?"

Emman said he would ask someone to go there, and she thanked him before she ended the call, glad for the support.

With her phone still in her hand, Stella went online to search for the hospital with the hope to get a phone number she could call but the name did not come up. She became more agitated. What kind of hospital was it? She hoped Chris would not be mismanaged there, and that she would find him alive.

Next, she called Mercy and when the call was picked, she said, "Mercy, please pray! Pray!"

"Stella, what happened?!" Mercy asked.

"It's Chris!"

"Chris?! What happened to him?" Mercy asked. She hoped Stella would not say that the man she saw just on Saturday was dead.

"Someone called and told me that Chris was involved in an accident. I don't know how he is. Please pray!"

"I will. Please calm down and keep praying. The Lord is on the throne. He will help us in Jesus' name."

They were still talking when Stella's phone began to beep. Moving it away from her ear, she checked and found that it was an unknown number. Suspecting that it might be related to the issue at hand, she decided to answer it.

She told Mercy that she had an incoming call, ended the call with Mercy, and answered the incoming call. It was indeed related to the accident; it was from the hospital. The caller confirmed that Chris was in the hospital and a doctor was already attending to him to save his life but his family would need to deposit some money for his treatment.

"Okay. How much?"

The female voice told Stella the amount required.

"Okay, I will -" Stella was about to ask that the hospital's bank account details should be forwarded to her so she could transfer the money right away, but she stopped and changed her mind. What if it was a scam? She would like to get to the hospital first and see Chris before she paid the money.

She started again. "I'm on my way to the hospital already, and will be there soon. Continue the treatment please, I will give you the money."

She hoped that the lady at the other end would agree, and was relieved when she did.

"Please don't delay." The lady added.

When the call ended, Ade asked, "Was that from the hospital?"

"Yes." Stella answered, and said that they would need to get to an ATM machine so she could withdraw some cash.

On the way to the nearest bank, she called one of Chris' very close friends to inform him. He said he would come to the hospital and also send someone to the accident scene to retrieve Chris' vehicle.

At a bank, Ade stopped the car and Stella alighted. There were three ATM machines with one free for her to use. She went there and withdrew the amount of cash that was needed. She quickly returned to the car, and they continued the journey to the hospital.

She called her mother and asked her to pray, but that she should not call Chris' parents as they were yet to be informed.

Just as the call ended, her pastor's wife called to know if she had reached the hospital, and she said she was almost there.

Within minutes, Ade and Stella reached their destination and Stella saw that the hospital looked decent—better than she had thought.

As soon as the car stopped, she opened her door, and slid out of the passenger seat before Ade had cut the ignition. The front of the hospital had been decorated for Christmas, but she hardly noticed the beautiful decoration as she rushed inside the building with her colleague behind her.

Two nurses were at the nurses' desk. Stella asked for Nurse Mariam and was told that she was busy.

Ade explained to the nurses that they learned that some accident victims had been brought in and that Stella's husband was among them. He mentioned the name and the nurses confirmed that it was true.

"I need to see him!" Stella pleaded with them.

"Okay, hold on."

Just then, a nurse emerged from a room and came in their direction. When she reached them, one of the two nurses told her that the visitors would like to see one of the accident victims.

"The doctor is still attending to him. You won't be able to see him now."

"Is he okay?" Stella wanted to know.

"I don't know. Only the doctor can tell."

She told Stella that she would need to pay some money as deposit for her husband's treatment, and then directed her to the cashier.

Ade followed Stella and after making the payment, they were asked to wait in a waiting room. There, Stella glanced at the people who sat and as they looked back at her, she could see scowls on the faces of some of them. She wondered what brought them to the hospital. Some others had anxious expectation in their eyes, which she was certain was in her eyes too. One man clutched his hands in a fist while a woman was pacing the floor. Stella had never liked coming to hospitals, and if someone had told her that she would be here today, she would have said it was impossible.

Some empty seats were on a side, and Stella and Ade went over to sit. She looked down as she continued praying. When the door opened, she looked up. A male nurse entered, went to a couple to speak with them, and left.

Within twenty minutes, Stella and Ade were joined by two pastors from the church, and Chris' brother, Emman. Shortly after, Chris' friend and a colleague joined them in the waiting room.

Glancing around the room, Emman said that they might need to move Chris to another hospital as he didn't think that this hospital had the level of care or services that Chris might need, and the others agreed.

"But we need to see him first to know the full seriousness of his condition." Chris' friend added.

Some minutes after, a nurse entered, glanced at the people around and called out, "Chris Brume?"

Stella and the others with her stood immediately and went to the nurse.

"Yes, I'm his wife." Stella said. "How is he?"

"He's in a critical condition, but he's alive."

"I need to see him please!"

"Yes, please come."

Emman spoke. "I'm his brother, and these are -" he looked from the two pastors to the other three men, "Pastors from his church and his friends. Can we all go with her?"

The nurse hesitated, and then shook her head. "No. Only his wife and maybe one other person. Only two visitors at a time."

"But when I was coming in, I was told that there are no visiting hours and families can come at any time." Chris' friend said with a frown.

"Yes, that's true but because of his condition, we can't allow too many people." The nurse explained.

She eventually conceded that Chris' brother and one of the pastors could go with Stella.

As they left the waiting room, Stella asked the nurse if she was Mariam and when she said yes, she asked for Chris' phone. Mariam produced it from her pocket and gave it to her.

They reached a door which the nurse opened and entered. Stella peered from behind the nurse and when she saw that someone was on an examination table, she entered the room and the two men followed. A nurse stood by the head of the examination table, monitoring the vital signs of the person on it.

Without a word to the nurses, Stella and the two men went straight to the still body on the examination table to look at the face. It was indeed Chris.

The shirt and trousers that he wore in the morning were still on him, but they were now very dirty and soaked with blood. He had an IV in one arm.

"Chris?!" Stella shouted and burst into tears.

"Satan is a liar!" The pastor declared and began to speak in tongues under his breath.

Mariam explained that Chris was brought in unconscious.

As soon as she stopped talking, the pastor asked Stella and Emman to begin to pray. Placing their hands on Chris, they began to pray for divine intervention and that Chris would live.

"Please, lower your voices." Mariam told them before she left the room and closed the door.

They were still praying fifteen minutes after when the door opened and a doctor came in. They stopped praying, greeted him, and moved away from Chris to allow the doctor to attend to him.

The doctor checked the chart by the examination table, examined Chris, and asked the nurse some questions. Turning to Stella and the others, he ascertained who they were before he began to explain Chris' condition to them. He also made them know the things he had done and the things that would still need to be done in order to save Chris' life.

When they asked if Chris would be alright, he answered, "Well, there are no guarantees at this point because he's in a critical condition. There's no way to know yet but let's be hopeful."

Chris' brother said he'd like to have a word with him, and he followed the doctor out of the room.

Stella began to cry again.

"Don't cry, the Lord is in control." The pastor told her.

Just then, the pastor's phone began to ring. He answered it, and then held the phone out to Stella. "It's the senior pastor."

She collected it and when she told the senior pastor about Chris' condition, the pastor said the program had just ended, and that he and his wife would be at the hospital soon.

Stella thanked him, ended the call, and returned the phone to the owner.

Shortly after, the pastor said he would go to the waiting room to join his colleague in order to await the arrival of the senior pastor and his wife.

CHAPTER 4

STELLA CARRIED A chair that was in a corner of the room, brought it to where Chris was, and sat down. Placing a hand on Chris, she began to declare God's words on him again. "You will live and not die! You will regain consciousness! I will not become a young widow, in Jesus' name." She also told him that she loved him.

When Chris' boss called her and she said that Chris was unconscious, he was alarmed, and told her that he would come over as soon as he could.

Emman returned to the room while talking on the phone, and from what he was saying, Stella knew that he was talking to his parents. When the call ended, he confirmed to Stella that he had informed his parents about Chris and that they would join them soon.

He also said that the people who were asked to go to the accident scene reported that Chris' SUV had been towed to a police station before their arrival. He had asked them to go to the police station.

Not long after, the senior pastors arrived, prayed for Chris, and began to speak with Stella and Emman to know how the accident happened.

They were still talking when the door opened and Chris' parents rushed in. His mother was crying, and the senior pastors encouraged them not to panic, but to pray. Some minutes after, the pastors left.

The visitors who had been in the waiting room were eventually permitted to see Chris but only for a few minutes. More family members which included Stella's parents, friends, and colleagues arrived.

Two policemen also came. While talking to Stella and Chris' family members, they revealed that the driver of the bus which caused the accident was drunk and unlicensed. He had been arrested and would subsequently be charged to court.

"We don't know for sure why Chris did not see the driver ... he was most likely distracted ... probably using his phone or doing something that distracted him. We also saw food in his car." They said.

They asked Stella to write a statement which she did, and then they left.

The family began to discuss on the next line of action to save Chris' life, and they agreed that he should be moved to a particular hospital.

"Are you sure that the hospital is good?" Chris' mother asked her first son, Emman.

"Oh yes. It's one of the best around." He said without hesitation. It's got some specialists, and it's better equipped to treat Chris. He will be in good hands."

With that decided, they began to make calls. Emman, Chris' friend, and one of Chris' colleagues went to the doctor in charge of Chris to talk to him.

At about three-fifteen that afternoon, Mercy, and Mercy's friend, Lekan arrived. Few minutes after, Stella's colleague, Ade, said that he'd have to return to the office, and she thanked him for his support. He wanted to know if she would want her car to be brought to her in the hospital or taken to her house, and when she said she preferred the hospital, he promised to get one of the company's drivers to bring it that evening.

Shortly after, her phone began to ring. It was an unknown number, but she answered it. "Hello,"

"This is Dr. Abel Kanu. I called you in the morning to inform you about your husband."

"Oh, good afternoon." She checked the phone to be sure that the number he was calling on showed on her screen. "Thank you so much. I would have called you, but I realized that I didn't have your number. You used my husband's phone to call me."

"Yes, I know, but even if you had my number, I would not expect you to call under this circumstance. Have you seen your husband? How's he?"

She explained that she was with him, but he was unconscious. She also told him what the policemen said.

Abel wanted to know if she had collected Chris' phone from Mariam, and she said she had. He asked her to hope for the best and before the call ended, she thanked him again for his call and concern.

Mercy asked Stella if she had eaten at all and when she said no, Mercy and Lekan left and went to a restaurant across the road to get food for her and snacks for the others. Stella accepted the food but couldn't eat much. Chris' and Stella's parents declined. How could they eat when their son was between life and death?

At about five, more friends and families which included Lola's mother arrived, and around six, Stella's car was brought to the hospital.

Her boss also came. When she explained that she would not be able to come to work for some days, he said he understood, and asked her to request for some days off. She promptly requested for two weeks and it was immediately approved.

Necessary arrangements were made and by eight-thirty that evening, Chris was on a stretcher in an ambulance, on his way to *Beacon Memorial Hospital.* Stella and the people who were still around followed in their cars. A medical team had been waiting at the hospital, and as soon as Chris arrived, he was taken to the emergency unit.

One of the doctors attending to him came to his family in the intensive care unit waiting room where they sat and explained that series of tests and an emergency surgery would have to be carried out. They gave their consent.

Shortly after, some of the visitors left with a promise to come the next day.

At about eleven, the remaining visitors were ready to leave— Mercy, Lekan, and Stella's parents. Emman said that he would stay back with Stella, and that his parents could leave too. His mother wanted to stay but others prevailed on her to go home.

"There's not much for you to do." Emman added. "There's no point staying when Chris is not conscious yet."

Reluctantly, the woman agreed to leave with her husband and when she said she would be back early the next day, Emman asked her to bring food for him and Stella.

Chris was eventually brought back and taken into an intensive care unit. Two comfortable chairs were in the unit and Emman sat in one. Stella put the second chair next to Chris' bed and sat down.

A medium size TV on the wall was showing some breaking news on a news channel.

"Can I turn this off?" Emman asked Stella with a grimace. "What we need at this time is God's word, not this."

Stella agreed and it was turned off.

She was beyond exhaustion, yet she couldn't sleep because she wasn't comfortable on the chair. Also, she had a lot on her mind. Why didn't Chris see the vehicle? Was he indeed doing something that distracted him as the police and Abel said? What exactly was he doing?

Then she counselled herself that this was not a time to get upset or to think about what went wrong. What Chris needed now was divine intervention.

Brushing aside her troubling musings, she began to pray again, "Chris, you will not die. You will overcome this in Jesus' name."

All through the night, nurses came in at intervals to check on Chris.

Stella eventually fell asleep and woke up around six-thirty in the morning when a nurse entered the room. Emman also woke up.

When Chris' parents arrived about half an hour after, carrying two big plastic bags, Stella and Emman stood to greet and relieve them of the bags. As they put the bags down, Emman's mother mentioned the items in the bags: bowls of food; four bottles of water; toothbrushes; and a toothpaste. She and her husband had stopped on their way to the hospital to buy them.

Standing by Chris' bed, the couple wanted to know if there had been any improvement since they left and what the doctors said. Stella and Emman answered.

They prayed for Chris and then sat on the chairs that Stella and Emman had vacated.

Now hungry, Stella took toothbrush and toothpaste, and headed for the visitors' restroom. Within minutes, she was back in the room and as she got her food, she thanked her parents-in-law for it. Then she sat on a side of the floor to eat, and Emman did the same.

Stella was still eating when she received a call on WhatsApp from her cousin, Lola. Lola revealed that she was calling from Dubai where she and her husband, John, were, for their honeymoon. John, who was apparently beside her, greeted Stella and said that they had just learned that Chris had an accident.

Clearly surprised and concerned, they asked, "How is he now?"

When Stella answered that he was still unconscious, they prayed for him and promised to call again soon.

At about ten that morning, Chris was taken away for a second round of tests and treatment while his family members waited in his room.

Stella took the remote control and sat on the edge of his bed. While searching available channels, she stumbled on a Christian channel which was playing a song at the time. *Good.* This would minister to everyone in the room while they waited for Chris to be returned, she thought as she put the remote control down.

The song ended and a Christmas song began to play—Joy *to the world the Lord is come.*

Hmm, Christmas. Stella sighed. She hoped Chris would survive this attack of the devil. She hoped he would regain consciousness and be discharged before Christmas Day, which was seventeen days away. She and Chris had made plans for their first Christmas together, and she had bought Christmas gifts for him. She hoped he would recover quickly so they could return home to their normal lives.

But what if he didn't make it?! She wondered and shuddered. She couldn't even bring herself to consider that. He just had to survive. God would see him through, she prayed under her breath.

Feeling sleepy after some minutes, she got up from the bed and returned to the floor. She rested against the wall, made herself comfortable, and soon dozed off.

She woke up when her parents arrived. Two of Chris' friends also joined them in the room. Shortly after, Emman said that his attention was needed in his office, and he left.

The tests took some time and by the time Chris was brought back to the room, the two friends had left.

Feeling both dirty and drained of energy, Stella decided to go home. What she needed now was a shower and rest. She would also need to take some necessities. She wasn't sure that she'd be able to rest though, as she had to be back in hospital as soon as possible. She would like to be there whenever Chris regained consciousness.

She announced her plan to her parents and parents-in-law, and after ensuring that Chris was comfortable in bed, she left.

At home, she ate a little, had a shower, and wore fresh clothes. She also took some necessities and on the way back to the hospital, she stopped at a store to buy two blankets. She and whoever decided to stay back in the hospital could put the blankets on the floor to sleep, she reasoned.

Back at the hospital, she saw some church members in Chris' room, and she thanked them for coming. Few minutes after, her parents and the church members left, while some other people arrived, including Lola's mother, Mercy and her husband, Dayo. Mercy brought bowls of rice, fish stew, and vegetable soup which Stella appreciated. That would be dinner for her and whoever was around at the time that she would eat.

Abel called Stella in the evening, and she told him that Chris had been moved to another hospital but that he was still unconscious. When she mentioned the name of the hospital—*Beacon Memorial Hospital*—he said that it was not far from where he worked.

"I'll try to stop by tomorrow." He promised.

Chris' brother returned around eight in the evening and about an hour later, his parents and the visitors who were around left.

Stella told Chris' brother that she bought two blankets that they could put on the floor so that they could sleep better. However, he declined and said that he'd manage on the chair.

When she was ready to sleep around ten, she put a blanket on the floor, wrapped herself with it, and was soon fast asleep.

By seven-thirty on Wednesday morning, Chris' parents were back in the hospital and Chris' brother left. Stella's parents-in-law sat on the chairs while Stella stood.

At about nine, some of Chris' colleagues and church members joined them in the room. Standing in the middle of the room, the church members began to pray for Chris.

CHAPTER 5

CHRIS COULD HEAR some people's voices around him. He wanted to talk to them, but somehow, he couldn't. To get the people's attention, he tried to move, but couldn't and he wondered why. *What's going on? Where am I?*

He had to do something to get their attention, and he decided to try again, but it was the same. Well, if his body would not move, he would move his hand, he told himself. Even if it was a finger, he must try to move it. He didn't know why but somehow, getting those people's attention was important to him. He needed to make them know that he was there.

****

As Chris' mother prayed with the others for Chris, she did not close her eyes. Her eyes were on her son. Suddenly, she noticed that his hand moved slightly.

"I think his hand moved just now!" She shouted.

"His hand?!" Stella asked.

"Yes!" His mother confirmed.

They all stopped what they were doing and came near him in bed.

Stella touched his shoulder. "Chris? Chris, can you hear me?"

They watched him closely for a sign, but there was no sound or movement.

"His hand moved, I'm sure of it." His mother insisted.

"Chris? We are here. We love you. If you can hear me, move your hand again. Do something to make us know that you can hear me." Stella told him. "Wake up in Jesus' name!"

Some of the people in the room were speaking in tongues while they continued watching him.

For some minutes there was nothing. And then a finger moved slightly again.

"Oh, thank You Jesus!" Stella shouted.

"Please call a nurse!" His mother said to one of the church members.

****

Chris heard louder voices.

Someone touched him, and a voice was calling Chris and asking him to move his hand again. He thought that the voice sounded familiar, but he wasn't sure.

Also, he wasn't sure if the person was talking to him but yes, he could move his hand a little.

And when he did it again, he heard more shouting and some of them calling Chris. Who was Chris? Was that him?

When someone said 'Please call a nurse!' he wondered where he was. *The nurse?! What's happening to me?*

He needed to see who these people were, and his eyes flickered open.

He heard more shouting. Confused, he glanced around blankly. He would have loved to see the faces of the people shouting but still feeling sleepy and weak, he closed his eyes and slept back.

He didn't know how long he slept, but he suddenly started hearing voices again, and he opened his eyes again.

The light in the room was bright and he had to adjust his eyes. He could see some people looking down at him, and as he stared at them, he didn't think he recognised any of them. One of them was calling Chris and asking how he was feeling. He guessed that the person was a doctor or a nurse, but he did not respond as he stared back.

After a thorough examination, the person began to give certain instructions to someone, and just then, Chris' eyes drifted close again.

Another person began to call Chris again. It was the familiar voice and this time, he opened his eyes and decided to respond. "Yes."

"It's me, Stella, your wife."

Stella? Still looking at the face hovering over him, he suddenly recognised her. *Ah*!

"Stella," he whispered her name.

"Yes, Chris. How are you feeling?"

He didn't know how he was feeling, so he didn't answer.

"Daddy and Mommy are also here." Stella told him and then moved back to allow them come near him.

He stared at them for a moment before recognising them. When they asked how he felt, he simply nodded.

They were trying to talk to him, but he didn't feel like talking yet. He needed to understand why he was here, and he closed his eyes again.

Why am I here? Am I dead or alive?

He opened his eyes again, and when he saw his mother, he asked in a weak voice, "Am I in a hospital?"

"Yes."

"Am I dead or alive?"

She smiled, "You're alive!"

Alive. He was happy to hear that. "What happened to me?"

"You had an accident."

An accident?! He closed his eyes again to think, but he didn't remember the accident.

He was still thinking when a doctor came into the room to check him. He was followed by a nurse. The doctor wanted to know if Chris had symptoms of some hidden problems aside the obvious ones and he answered the doctor's questions. The doctor carefully evaluated him and gave instructions to the nurse.

When they left, Stella came near Chris and he asked her, "When did the accident happen?"

"On Monday morning, three days ago."

"So, I've been here for three days?!"

"Yes."

Three days! That shocked and bothered him.

Stella saw the look on his face and told him, "You'll be fine and discharged soon. Everything will be alright."

As Chris asked more questions and thought about the answers that he received, he searched his brain to connect them. Suddenly, he remembered the accident.

"I remember the accident." He said in a whisper.

"Do you remember how it happened?"

He nodded. "I remember that I was driving. Maybe I wanted to make a call or send a message, and then the vehicle came out of nowhere. I wanted to avoid it, but it suddenly hit my car."

Stella wanted to blame him for using his phone while driving, but stopped. That would not achieve anything. God had delivered him. He had regained consciousness and that was the most important thing.

He wanted to know where his SUV was and was told that it had been towed to his brother's office.

****

At about three-thirty in the afternoon, Stella went home to take some things and returned to the hospital around six. Entering the building, she walked down the hallway to where the elevator was, and pressed the up button.

While she waited for it, a well-dressed man approached and when he got to her, he said hello with a smile, and she responded briefly. The elevator came and they both entered it. He selected the third button, looked at her to know her floor, and she said it was the same floor. The doors of the elevator closed and they didn't talk again until they reached the floor.

They got off the elevator and while she went in the direction of Chris' room, the man approached the nurses' desk to make enquiries.

In the room, Chris was not in bed and she was told that he had been taken away for a test.

She was still putting away the items she brought from home when there was a light knock on the door and it opened. She looked up and saw the well-dressed man. Surprised, she thought that he must be one of Chris' colleagues.

"Hello." The man greeted generally and glanced at the faces of the people in the room briefly.

They responded and waited to know who he was.

"I am Dr. Abel Kanu."

What?! "Oh, Dr. Abel!" Stella said and stepped forward. "I am Stella, Chris' wife."

Abel smiled broadly as he shook hands with Stella. "When we got down at the same floor, it occurred to me that you might be Chris' wife but I wasn't sure. I'm sorry that we're meeting under this circumstance."

Stella looked at Chris' parents and introduced Abel. "He's the one who called me to inform me about the accident."

Chris' parents and brother greeted Abel well and thanked him for all that he did.

"Where is your husband?" Abel asked Stella.

She told him that he had been taking away for a test and should be back soon.

He consulted his wristwatch briefly, and said, "Okay. I'll wait at the reception. I need to make one or two calls."

"Alright. I'll let you know when he returns." She said. "He has regained consciousness."

"Oh, awesome!" He responded and flashed a grin before he left the room.

About fifteen minutes after, Chris returned to the room. The nurse got him in bed, made him comfortable, and left.

Stella told Chris about Abel, and that Abel was waiting to see him. Then she went outside to call Abel.

He was on the phone, but when he looked up and saw her approaching, he asked, "Is he back?"

"Yes."

"I'll talk to you later." He said into the phone, stood, and followed her.

In the room, he went to Chris with a broad smile. He made Chris know that he had witnessed the accident, and he revealed all that he knew about it.

"The scene was like something out of a movie." Abel added. "As a matter of fact, you shouldn't have survived the accident. It was nothing short of a miracle."

"Thank You, Jesus!" Chris' parents said.

Chris thanked Abel for all that he had done, and when Abel was ready to leave, Chris' brother saw him off to the elevator.

Two days after, on Friday morning, the medical director came into the room to let them know the results of some of the tests carried out and the situation of things. The family wanted to know why Chris did not seem to have feelings in his legs and had not been able to move them. He answered their questions and when they asked if Chris would be able to walk again, he said it was possible, but he was not very sure if Chris would make a full recovery. He told them that a CT scan would have to be done to determine the extent of the damage.

As the medical director talked, Stella glanced at Chris and saw what looked like fear in his countenance. When the doctor left, she assured Chris that he would be fine and that she and many others were praying for him.

Stella and the others began to pray that Chris would have a speedy recovery and walk again.

When Abel visited again on Saturday, she told him what the medical director said about Chris, and he encouraged her to be optimistic.

A nurse who had been very pleasant to Chris and his family came into the room to check on Chris. Whenever she came, she always had something funny to say to brighten the mood in the room.

Before she left, Chris asked her, "Do you think that I'll walk again?"

"Maybe ... I don't know. The doctor will confirm soon." Then she smiled, "Just focus on getting better and in no time, everything will be fine. You're in good hands here."

There was no assurance in her words, but it was not a definite no, and he decided to be hopeful. He would also pray.

Everyone continued praying for him as he was taken away for CT scan on Monday.

Two days after, the medical director was back in the room and looking serious.

Why was he looking like a bearer of bad news? Stella wondered.

As the man began to talk, Stella held her breath, hoping it would be good news. It had to be. She and Chris were Christians. It just wasn't possible that her husband would not walk again.

As he talked, no one took note of the Christmas song playing in the background. They were more interested in what the man had to say.

Stella waited for the medical director to get to the point.

Finally, after much analysis which Stella didn't really understand, the doctor said in clear lay terms that Chris' spinal cord had been affected.

He looked directly at Chris and explained, "Some nerves are heavily damaged in his spinal cord."

Spinal cord?! Heavily damaged?! What was he trying to say, Stella wondered with a frown.

She didn't have to wait for long as the man went on and revealed, "I'm sorry, but I don't think you will ever walk again."

"Not walk again?!" Everyone in the room exclaimed almost at the same time.

Wha-t?! Stella looked at the man in both disbelief and shock.

Others in the room looked stunned too and, for some seconds, no one talked as they tried to process the information.

Then the questions started coming. Everyone was obviously devastated by the news, including Chris. They knew that not walking again was a possibility, but they hadn't expected it. They had been hopeful.

As some of the others began to ask the doctor questions and he answered, Stella seemed frozen where she was standing. She still struggled to process the information in her brain. *Does that mean Chris will be in a wheelchair for the rest of his life*?! *Aahhh*!

"No!" She suddenly said and shook her head. This couldn't be happening. This must be a bad dream, and she hoped that she would wake up soon.

While the medical director explained things to Chris and his family, Stella stared at him, still unable to believe what she'd just heard.

She glanced in Chris' direction and saw that his face had crumbled with some deep emotion which seemed more like fear.

When the doctor left, the family discussed and decided to get some other doctors opinions.

That night, Stella couldn't sleep. As she continued thinking about the implications of what the medical director explained, she realized that Chris might not be able to make love to her again. And then it occurred to her that he might not be able to father a child. *Lord have mercy*!

She suddenly became angry at Chris. How could he have been using the phone to text while driving? How could he have allowed this to happen? She eventually slept around three in the morning.

Later in the day, another doctor came and began to explain some of the implications of a spinal cord injury. He added that the injury had impacted Chris' bladder and bowel.

Stella had some questions which were begging for answers. However, she couldn't ask in the presence of everyone—especially Chris—and when the doctor was leaving, she followed him.

In his office, she asked the doctor if Chris would be able to father a child. In response, he explained about the damage to his body again, and then said that it was unlikely. His sexual functions had also been affected.

She broke down. "Is there nothing that can be done?! Our marriage is not up to a year ... we don't even have a child yet! We agreed to start a family after a year."

The doctor said that there was nothing that could be done.

 CHAPTER 6

ON THE WAY home later to shower, Stella was crying. It was obvious that they would spend Christmas in the hospital. She could deal with that. However, she didn't think that she could deal with the bad news which she had just received. This was not what she had planned. This was not how they had thought that they would spend their first Christmas together. This was not what she had expected in her marriage.

She suddenly remembered that she was supposed to resume at work on Tuesday. She called her boss and told him that she would not be able to return to work on that day, and that she should be given till the first week of the New Year. She applied for extra days and was approved.

Friends and family began to consult with some other medical doctors to get help for Chris. *This can't happen to him.*

They showed some doctors the results of Chris' tests, and by the twenty forth of December, all the doctors had responded. They were of the same opinion ... Chris' life had been changed.

Our lives have been changed, Stella thought, weeping.

As she lay on the hospital floor that Christmas Eve, wrapped in her blanket, she was still trying to get her head around the fact that their lives had been altered. She hadn't thought that this could happen—but it had.

What next? What would happen to Chris' plans? Her plans? Their plans?! Their marriage?! She continued thinking, and weeping, and asking God for a miracle until she slept around four in the morning.

She woke up about three hours later, on Christmas Day, but didn't feel like getting up. She almost couldn't believe that she was where she was on Christmas Day—on the floor of a hospital room. Knowing that families and friends would visit, she dragged her wearied body up, freshened up, and wore a simple yellow dress.

At about ten-thirty, friends and family members began to arrive. Some of them were obviously coming from church.

A few of them brought food and drinks, while others brought Christmas gifts for Chris, his parents, and Stella.

When they asked Chris to change from his hospital dressing gown to a nice shirt so that they could take pictures with him, he refused. They also wanted to turn on the TV to brighten up his mood, but he said no.

Stella came to him. "Let us turn the TV on. It's Christmas Day."

"I said no!" He snapped at her.

She took a deep breath and tried again, "Chris, it's Christmas Day—"

"I don't care! You can leave if you'd rather be somewhere else!" He said rudely.

"Chris, calm down!" One of them told him.

As Stella stepped away from Chris, another person came to her, put a hand on her shoulder, and told her in a whisper, "Don't let what he said upset you. He's going through a lot right now."

In the evening, Stella decided to go home to sleep. She couldn't sleep on the hospital floor tonight. She needed to think. Going home to sleep and rest for the first time since Chris had the accident almost three weeks ago might help her to calm down and get a grip. She felt like she was losing her mind.

She told Chris' parents and brother of her decision, and they said that they understood.

She came to stand by Chris' bed. "I'll be back tomorrow morning."

He told her she could leave. "I don't need you!" He added, rage obviously mixing with grief.

His brother and father asked him to calm down, but his mother was silently weeping and asking God for a miracle for him.

At home, Stella sat in the living room and looked at the Christmas tree. She didn't bother to plug in the lights on the tree. What was there to celebrate? She thought.

Suddenly feeling overwhelmed, she went into their bedroom, flung herself on the bed and began to cry. "Why us, Lord?! Why did this happen?" She asked aloud but didn't seem to hear a thing.

She eventually got up to eat and shower. She returned to the bedroom, and as she prepared to sleep alone in bed for the first time since they got married, she started weeping again. This was going to be hard for her.

When she woke up in the morning, she sat by the window of their bedroom, looking out, thinking, and talking to God.

How could this have happened? How could something that had been going right suddenly go wrong? *Lord, I don't understand!*

****

In the hospital, Chris was also asking God some questions. For a long time, he couldn't sleep as he kept thinking.

He remembered what happened to a friend's brother when he had stroke. His wife left him with the children!

And ... did it mean that sex with Stella was lost?! He and Stella did not even have a child yet. If sex was lost, how could he expect her to stay with him? Stella was just twenty seven years old.

He had also heard about a wife who was having sex with one of her husband's friends because her husband could no longer be intimate with her due to paralysis. When the husband got to know about it and confronted her, she left him and left their only child with him.

Chris wondered what to do.

He had lost the use of his legs. Sex with his wife was lost. He had lost all hope and plans to have children. He had also lost his dignity as the male nurses who attended to him saw his nakedness frequently.

Also, with the look of things, he would lose even his marriage and job.

Tears streamed down his face silently when he realized the extent of it.

It seemed that he had lost everything. *At the age of thirty!* He would have to rely on other people to do some things for him!

As he thought about the extent of his challenge, he decided that he would commit suicide. What was there to live for? He didn't want to live like this! He would not want to become a burden. He was an active person. Rather than become dependent and live in a wheelchair for the rest of his life, he'd rather die, he reasoned.

All hope was gone. No hope for him.

As he pondered about this, he could hear a voice deep down in his spirit telling him to remain hopeful. However, he didn't want to hear the voice as he focused on his feelings and situation. How could God allow this to happen to him? Not once had it ever crossed his mind that he could be like this.

He was still thinking when he eventually fell asleep.

When Stella returned to the hospital the day after Christmas, she was told that Chris didn't sleep for a long time. So, she allowed him to continue to sleep.

One of Chris' very close friends arrived and stood on a side.

Chris eventually woke up and she went to him. A look at her told him that like him, she must have been crying and probably had a sleepless night. Her eyes were red and puffy.

She greeted him. "How are you?"

But he did not respond. *She will leave me soon*, he thought. Tears sprang to his eyes and he looked away.

"Chris?"

"Leave me alone! How do you think I am?" He snapped.

Stella stepped back.

His friend came to him to encourage him. "Don't do that, Chris. This is the time to draw close to your wife and fight a common enemy."

He did not respond.

"Chris," Stella called him again and touched his shoulder.

He couldn't hold his emotion back anymore and tears began to pour down his face.

"Oh, Chris, no!" His friend said.

Stella began to cry. She reached out to take his hand, but he pulled away from her. She remained where she was and continued crying.

His parents, who were present also began to cry.

As the friend wiped away Chris' tears, he stated, "We have to trust God, Chris. And don't forget that when there's life, there's hope. It could have been worse. You could have died, but God saved you."

"Why didn't I die? Why didn't God kill me?" Chris responded angrily. "Is it not better to have died than to be like this?"

"No. Please don't say that. We are glad that you're alive."

Stella stepped away and others came to Chris to talk to him, but he did not respond.

He didn't want to talk. It was easy for them to talk—to say that everything would be alright. However, he didn't see how everything would be alright. His life had been altered, he thought.

Stella slept on the hospital room floor that night.

The next day, Sunday, when Chris' brother and friend arrived, she said that she had to get some things at a store and would be back soon.

When she left, Chris' brother and friend brought the two chairs in the room to his bedside and sat to talk to him.

"Chris, let's trust God." Emman told Chris.

The friend said, "We know how hard this is, but you have to encourage yourself."

Chris began to cry again. "How can I be in a wheelchair for the rest of my life? I'm just thirty! I celebrated my thirtieth birthday about three months ago!" He paused, and then added, "No, no, I don't want to be in a wheelchair. I don't want to become a burden to anyone. I'd rather die!"

"Don't think that way," His friend urged.

"Why not? What do I have left to offer anyone or the world? What's there to live for?" He said angrily.

"We understand how you feel. It's hard but you need to be strong. Be strong for yourself, your parents, and your wife—"

"Wife?" Chris made a sound. "I don't have a wife anymore."

"You have a wife. Stella is your wife." They pointed out.

"You think that she will want to stay?" He asked with arched brows.

They hesitated before they answered, "We think that she will stay."

"Well, she won't ... I'm telling you that right now!" He insisted. "Why should she stay?! What do I have to offer her?"

They took a deep breath as they considered his words.

He went on. "Which woman in her right senses will want to be with a man in this situation?"

"A woman who fears the Lord and loves her husband." His friend answered.

He snorted. "Do you even understand?! No more sex! No child! No job! No legs!"

"Hold on ... have you lost your job already?" His friend asked.

"No, but I know that I will. Do you know what that means?" He said and paused.

Then he smiled sadly and added, "No, you don't know because you're not in my shoes."

He began to weep again as he said, "I can't even wear shoes anymore. All my shoes. All the shoes I have! My car!"

His brother couldn't respond as tears filled his eyes.

"I really don't understand why this happened, but I know that God is on the throne still. He's still in control." The friend insisted.

"What will happen to me?!" Chris asked. It was as if he did not hear what his friend said.

The friend told him that it would help to listen to sermons on healing and miracles, and to read the Bible. However, Chris' facial expressions showed that he wasn't listening to him.

They continued talking until Stella returned.

Some time later, Chris' younger brother, Luke, called him on WhatsApp, and as they spoke, Chris looked at his WhatsApp profile picture. It was of him and Stella. In the picture, they stood hand in hand outside the house that they lived in—smiling and obviously happy.

But he was no longer happy and, believing that Stella would leave him soon, he made a mental note to remove the picture and leave the space blank. As soon as the call ended, he removed the picture and put the phone down.

Stella took the remote control and turned the TV on to the Christian station, but Chris asked her to turn it off.

"Why?"

"I don't want to hear it." He answered without looking in her direction.

"But—"

"No!"

She turned it off and put the remote down. She tried to talk to him but he did not respond, and only talked when he needed her to do something for him.

He obviously didn't want to talk to her, and that was okay by her. She didn't feel like talking much as she had a lot on her mind. What was there to talk about, anyway?

****

Stella went home every day to shower and change clothes. Back in the hospital room, she sat down thinking, crying, using her phone or talking to whoever was in the room with her and Chris.

Everyday, doctors, nurses, and hospital staff, came in and out of Chris' room to attend to him.

Some of the families, friends, and church members who visited did things to help Stella and Chris without being asked. Some of them made financial donations while some others brought food which Stella put in the refrigerator or freezer at home for later. She had not been able to cook or buy groceries since the day of the accident.

They all tried to encourage Chris but he refused to be pacified. He was angry still.

People prayed for him, but he couldn't pray ... didn't want to pray.

Plus his marriage seemed to be collapsing. He and Stella were both unhappy and drifting apart, but they didn't know what to do. She had stopped trying to make conversations with him and he could sense that like him, she was angry at the situation.

The year ended and a new year began on Friday, but Chris remained in bed in the hospital room—in his hospital dressing gown.

****

On Sunday afternoon, the third of January, Stella was alone with Chris in the hospital room. She sat on a chair with her eyes closed and thought about her office. She would be resuming tomorrow, but how could she work with everything happening in her life? She wondered. She was physically and emotionally down. And spiritually ... she knew.

She had informed Chris and his family that she would go home in the evening so that she could rest and prepare to resume at work the next day. His family and close friends had made plans to take turns so that one person would stay in the hospital with Chris at night.

It was Emman's turn this night. He arrived around six in the evening and at about nine, Stella left.

At home, there was no more food in the refrigerator for her to eat and she decided to drink *gaari*—a coarsely processed meal from cassava root. She showered, got in bed, and slept through the night until the alarm went off at five the next morning. She decided to change the alarm time from five to six in the morning since she would not have to prepare breakfast for Chris. She eventually left the house at seven so that she could stop at a restaurant to eat before getting to the office.

At the office, some of her colleagues came to her and asked about her husband, while some looked at her with pity and avoided her.

When she closed in the evening, she went to the hospital to see Chris and stayed till ten-thirty.

# CHAPTER 7

STELLA WENT TO work the next morning, and on her way to the hospital in the evening, she sighed, deep in thought. Was this how she would spend the rest of her life ... with her taking care of Chris and talking with doctors and nurses about his health?

Soon, he would start using a wheelchair, and she would have to help him transfer to and from the wheelchair. From the look of things, she would have to schedule her life and activities around him and his needs, which would mean that she would not have many social activities any more.

Aside these concerns, he would lose his job. How would his needs be met? How would their house rent be paid? How would she cope?! Would they have to depend on the generosity of families and friends? Also, what would happen if she lost her job?!

As she deliberated on these things, her fear and anxiety grew.

She stayed in the hospital until around nine-twenty and at home later, she ate, showered, and got in bed. Feeling down emotionally, she slept without saying even a word to God. How could He have allowed this to happen to her? She brooded.

When she woke up in the middle of the night to use the bathroom, she turned on the room light. Back in bed few minutes after, she took her phone from her bedside table to check the time. It was one-fifty. She returned the phone and started thinking about her life and marriage again.

How could she stay in this marriage with the way things were? How could she put her life and plans on hold? *All my plans?! Plans to have children*?! How could she put everything on hold to take care of a man who would be in a wheelchair for the rest of his life?! And how would they cope financially?

Some people might expect her to stay with Chris, but somehow she felt that it would seem unfair to expect that from her. She was still young!

But why did God allow this to happen? Why me?

Her eyes went to their framed wedding photograph on the bedroom wall and, as she looked at it, she thought back to their wedding day.

After the solemnisation that day, she and Chris stood hand-in-hand outside the church building to take pictures. They were such a happy pair. Afterward, they headed for the reception venue and at the appropriate time, they made their grand entrance into the well-decorated hall, dancing joyfully. They were followed by the bridal train and friends who were also dancing. When the reception ended, they went to the guest house which they had booked for their honeymoon, accompanied by a few friends so that they could pray and give thanks to God for the wedding. On Monday afternoon, they were having lunch in the restaurant of the guest house, talking and laughing, when Tokunbo, a director of the guest house, came to their table and said that the guest house had a gift for them...

... Stella sighed and brought her mind back to the present.

"God, help me in Jesus' name!" She muttered a few times, and then slept back.

She woke up when the alarm rang at six and, hoisting her tired body from the bed, she dressed up and went to work.

****

A week later, on Monday, January eleven, Chris was moved from the ICU to one of the hospital's private rooms. Some therapists were assigned to him and soon, he began to learn how to live in a wheelchair and move his body. During the day, he was taken away for some hours for therapy and treatments.

****

On Saturday morning, January sixteen, Mercy and Lekan visited Stella at home before she left for the hospital.

Mercy was dark in complexion, curvaceous and of an average height. She worked at *Jones Cosmetics Manufacturing Company*, and sold clothes on the side.

Lekan who was slim, slightly light skinned, and of an average height, worked in a multinational life insurance, pensions, and asset management company.

"We know you will not have time to cook, so we brought food for you, that is enough to last for some days." They said and put some bowls of food on a table.

"You must be in the spirit. I was just thinking of stopping on my way to the hospital to buy food to eat. I definitely don't have time to cook. Everything has been a roller coaster." Stella said and thanked them.

She got a plate and spoon, served herself, and sat down to eat.

"You haven't taken down the Christmas tree and decorations." Lekan commented, looking at the tree.

"Do I have time for that ... with all that is going on?" Stella rolled her eyes and hissed.

"We can do it while you're eating." Mercy offered. "It won't take long."

"I wouldn't mind."

As Stella began to eat, Mercy and Lekan got up to work. Removing the lights and ornaments from the tree, they wrapped them in tissue paper and newspaper to prevent them from breaking, and then placed them in plastic bags. The tree was disassembled and put in a box that Stella provided. They also removed the ornaments hanging from the ceiling and put them in a bag.

When Stella finished eating, she put the remaining food in the freezer, and back in the living room, she put the plastic bags and box away.

They all sat down and continued talking.

Then Lekan asked her, "So, how are things going?"

Stella shrugged.

"With the way things are now, what are your plans? Have you and Chris talked?" Mercy asked her.

She shrugged again. "What's there to talk about?"

"Everything. Moving forward, providing care for him ... your marriage. Some decisions will have to be made." Mercy pointed out.

"He does not even talk to me." Stella revealed.

Mercy and Lekan were surprised. "He doesn't?"

"No. He doesn't talk to me at all. Even if I ask him a question, he ignores me, and if he decides to answer, he responds in monosyllables."

"Why?" Mercy demanded.

Stella shrugged again.

"Well, it's understandable. It's because of what he's going through. It must be hard on him." Lekan said. "Some of such people plunge into seclusion. It's not unusual."

Mercy took a deep breath. "Yes, it may be understandable, but it won't help in any way."

Lekan shook her head. "No, it won't."

"Well, I really don't know how we can move forward." Stella stated matter-of-factly.

"You will have to move forward, God will help you." Mercy told her.

"I don't know how." Stella repeated and shook her head. "This Chris is not the Chris whom I married. He can no longer play the role of a husband. I will have to be the one taking care of him."

"But it's only his lower part that's affected. He can talk and use his hands."

"Yes, but I didn't marry him for just those things. I married him to be my husband in every sense of the word."

"We understand, but Chris needs you." Lekan said.

"Please remember that he is still the same man you married ... the same man who had dreams and hopes of your life together. That hasn't changed." Mercy added in a pleading way.

Lekan nodded in agreement. "What happened was the work of the devil. It wasn't his fault."

"Yes, it wasn't his fault, but it wasn't my fault either." Stella said.

"No, it wasn't." Lekan responded. "We are simply saying that he needs you."

Because Stella didn't think that they would understand her feelings and concerns, she decided not to say much to them.

At work on Tuesday, a colleague came to her and said in no uncertain terms that she should leave Chris, relocate to another country, and remarry.

Because Stella had been thinking along that line, the counsel resonated with her. It made sense and she felt a little better.

The colleague went on, "Thank God that you don't have a child for him yet that you would have to consider."

Stella nodded in agreement and thanked the lady. This was what she might have to do.

On Friday evening, on her way to the hospital, her mother called to say that she would like to visit her at home the next morning before she went to the hospital.

When her mother arrived on Saturday morning, she wanted to know how Stella was holding up.

"Honestly, I don't know. I didn't see this coming." Stella confessed. This was her mother; she would understand.

She did. "I understand. God is still in control." Her mother said as she slowly nodded. "He has not lost control. He's still on the throne and because He's on the throne, it is well."

"Hmm, are you sure, Mommy?" Stella looked doubtful.

Her mother nodded slowly again. "Yes."

Stella took a deep breath and then sighed.

"Tell me what's on your mind." Her mother urged.

She hesitated for some seconds and then said, "Mom?"

"Yes?"

"Do you want to hear the truth?"

"Yes, that's why I am here."

Stella took a deep breath before she said, "I don't see how I can stay with Chris."

Her mother nodded in understanding. "It's hard, I know ... but ... if God wants you to stay, He will give you the grace that you need and you can do it."

Stella glared at her. "To stay?! Mom?!"

Slowly, her mother said, "You're my daughter, Stella, and I love you dearly."

Stella looked away.

Her mother went on. "I'd love to tell you to leave and start over. I wish I could but I ... I can't. I don't think that you should leave him."

"You don't think that I should leave him?!" Stella looked back at her mother. She knew that her mother might say this, but she had expected her to understand her feelings, support her, and encourage her to leave Chris. That was what some mothers would do. They would not even think twice about telling their daughters to divorce such a man and start afresh.

Stella spoke again, "How can you say that, Mom?!"

Her mother did not talk for a moment as she struggled with her emotions.

"I told you what the doctors said! Have you forgotten?" Stella asked her mother. "Chris can't father a child!"

"I know -"

"If you know, how then can you tell me to stay in such a marriage?"

"It's not me, Stella. It's what I believe God will want you to do."

"Does that mean that I won't have children, Mom?! Do you know what this means?! You won't have a grandchild from me?" Stella said as tears began to roll down her cheeks.

With tears in her eyes, her mother responded, "We will have to trust God for a way out."

"For a way out?! Okay." Stella said, smiled in a sad way, and made a sound as she looked away.

"And you can always adopt."

She looked back at her mother. "I can always adopt?! That's what you have to say?! Okay." She nodded and looked away again.

"I'm not a medical doctor. Both of you should talk to your doctors—there will be a way out."

She looked at her mother again. "Mom, this situation is not even just about having children. If I stay with Chris, I won't have a life anymore! I will become his sole caregiver! I will have to plan my time and activities around his needs! There will be no money! We will have to depend on people! I can't cope, Mom!"

"Stella,"

Stella burst into tears. "I can't do this!"

Her mother held her as her own tears flowed. "I understand, Stella."

"No, you don't!"

"I do. But the only thing to do now is to trust God." Her mother said gently. "Also, let me know whatever I can do to help you."

Stella looked at her. "What can you do, Mom? How much can you do? How much money do you have?"

"I will do whatever I can, to help you. Your father, and even your siblings ... we're all here for you. I'm praying for you."

Stella looked down and held her head in her hands. "Why me, Lord?" She began to cry again.

As her mother encouraged her, she argued. She eventually kept quiet. There was no point in arguing with her mother. She knew what she would do.

On the way to the hospital shortly after her mother had left, Stella mulled over her mother's words. Her mother had asked her to stay with Chris.

But would Chris do this for her if she was the one in his position? She wondered.

Well, she would make her decision. It was her life. Her mother was not in her shoes, so she would not understand. Mercy and Lekan were also not in her shoes.

The senior pastor visited Chris the next day in company of his personal assistant. When he was ready to leave, he told Stella that he'd like to talk to her. She followed him out of the room, and when they reached the waiting area, they sat down, away from the pastor's PA, and a woman who was there.

He began to encourage Stella to be prayerful and strong in this trying period. Referring to some Scriptures, he asked her to seek the face of God to be certain of His will for her life.

Stella respected him and trusted his opinion. He had proved himself to be a true man of God. However, when he counselled her to support Chris, she became upset. She told him some of the things that the doctors said about Chris, and he made her know that he was aware.

"Sir, what would you advise your daughter, Mimi, to do if she were to be in this situation?"

"What I would tell Mimi is what I've just told you. Besides, you're also my daughter." He said and smiled in an understanding way.

Stella took a deep breath. *Oh Lord, why have You sent the pastor to talk to me?*

The pastor went on. "What you're going through is difficult. It's not easy, and so no one should judge or criticise you. Whoever is doing that should put himself or herself in your shoe and see how it fits. This is not what you hoped for or prepared for. Things have changed, and I understand. What I am simply saying is that you need to seek to hear God and then do what you need to do. Trust God and you won't regret it."

The pastor eventually prayed for her and left with his personal assistant.

On Saturday morning, Stella was alone in the hospital room with Chris. He was in his wheelchair while she sat on a chair and used her phone, responding to some chats.

"Stella?"

She looked at him. "Yes?"

"I don't expect you to stay in this marriage." As he talked, he did not look at her.

He went on. "I'm offering to release you so that you can marry another man." He could sense the Holy Spirit telling him to stop, but he closed his heart and chose to please himself. He felt it was better this way. After all, there was no way she would want to stay with an invalid—a husband who would never walk again. The man that he used to be was gone forever.

Surprised, she stared at him as she considered his words and searched for the best way to respond.

Keeping his voice flat, he added, "You can leave, okay?" He wanted it settled quickly so she wouldn't spring a surprise on him later.

This was what Stella wanted—to be released—yet she could not bring herself to accept the offer. It was as if the Holy Spirit was holding her back.

Not very sure of what to say, she did not respond.

He looked at her and said with a scowl, "Okay?"

She didn't respond still as tears filled her eyes. *Why can't I say yes and end this ordeal?*

"I need your answer!" His scowl deepened.

She got up and left the room. The reception was empty and as she sat on a chair, she burst into tears. She would need to pray and think in order to make the right decision. However, she had been struggling to pray and think right since that fateful day in December.

"Lord, help me!"

She was still there when one of her friends arrived, and she led her to the room.

In the afternoon of the next day, Sunday, when she and Chris were alone in the room, he told her, "I want your response to what I told you yesterday."

"I know." She said quietly.

"I want it now!" He glared at her.

"You will get it soon."

As he stared at her, he wondered what her decision would be. If she'd like to leave his life, she should leave without delay so he would know that he was alone.

Shortly after, his parents and brother arrived, and Stella vacated her seat.

At about five, the doctor in charge of his care came into the room to check him. Afterward, he said that Chris might be discharged in the month of April or May depending on the progress he was making.

While explaining how to take care of him at home, the doctor told Stella that if the apartment in which they lived was not on the ground floor, they should consider moving to a ground floor because of his wheelchair.

"Move to a ground floor?!" Chris asked, surprised.

Stella was upset. Would they have to move out of their beautiful apartment? That had not occurred to her.

When the doctor left, Chris discussed with his family and they decided to start looking for another accommodation immediately.

Chris would also need assistance and they agreed to employ the service of a male nurse.

Another reality was that Chris and Stella would have to downsize as they had so many expenses. They might need to find a two-bedroom apartment.

Chris' parents asked Stella for her opinion, but she simply shrugged as she was feeling overwhelmed already. When would all these troubles be over?!

At home that night, Stella cried again. Her life kept spiralling out of control and she couldn't do anything about it. She liked control and organization but nothing was the same anymore. She had lost control and could not organize what was happening. It was indeed a roller coaster as she told Mercy and Lekan in her house a few weeks back.

Besides, she hated to move with all the hassles of packing and unpacking. It had taken her some time to arrange their apartment and make it beautiful, and now, they would be moving out!

And worse—to a smaller place! *Ah! This is too much, Lord!*

CHAPTER 8

CHRIS WAS ALSO thinking about everything.

In the night, he covered his face with his cover cloth and wept silently. How would his needs be met? If he was not careful, his life would be totally ruined, reduced to nothing.

He had been trying to stay away from God in anger, but now, he realized that he needed God more than ever before. What could he do without Him?

As he cried, he remembered the words of Jesus' disciples in the Bible ... *Jesus, to whom shall we go?*

Indeed, he had no other help. He couldn't and shouldn't stay away from God.

"Lord, help me!" He broke down. "Please, help me ... in Jesus' name!"

Realising that God was listening to his plea for help, he continued, "I'm sorry, Lord ... for getting angry at You." He apologised. "But my heart is broken. My feet and spinal cord are broken. My plans are broken. My marriage! My life! What else is left? Can You just take me home?"

He cried harder. "Fix my life or take me home, Lord!"

His brother, whose turn it was to be in the hospital with him that night, woke up and came to him. "Chris! Chris!"

Chris cried harder.

His brother held him.

Chris eventually became calm, and he asked his brother to go back to sleep.

While he waited for sleep to claim him, he thought about Stella. She had not given him an answer, but his ultimatum to her was the least of his worries now as he had bigger fish to fry. He would follow up later.

As he thought about Stella and his ultimatum, he felt God telling him to reconsider his stand.

He eventually apologised. "I'm sorry Lord, but how can I expect her to stay?"

He eventually slept and woke up around seven-thirty in the morning. It was the first day of February and some people sent new month prayers and greetings to him, but he ignored them all.

When his father arrived around nine, he told Chris that he and his wife had an idea concerning the accommodation issue. They had been building a three-bedroom bungalow at the back of the five-bedroom bungalow in which they lived and where Chris lived until he rented his apartment. Their plan was to rent out the new bungalow, and it had reached a certain level but they'd had to stop because of their finances.

His father went on. "Instead of raising money to rent another apartment, why don't we use whatever money we can raise to complete the bungalow for you ... that is if you and Stella wouldn't mind to live in the same compound with us? I can get a loan from my bank or sell one of my properties."

As he talked, he looked from Chris to Emman, and back to Chris. "It will be your own house."

Chris and his brother thought that it was a good idea.

"Another advantage is that it can be designed to accommodate the wheelchair and your needs. Ramps can be built so that the wheelchair can easily get in to the house."

Chris nodded in agreement.

"Your mother and I will also be available to support you and Stella." His father added.

"I like the idea, but we will need to discuss with Stella too." Emman said.

His father agreed, but Chris didn't think that Stella's opinion mattered much.

"She's your wife. You're going to live there together, so her opinion matters." His father said.

Yes, Chris knew that. However, he just did not see Stella choosing to stay with him.

Emman wanted to know how much money would be needed to complete the bungalow, and his father gave an estimate.

"I'll call Luke and discuss with him to see how much he can send." Emman said. "If Stella is in support of the idea, you can start with the money from Luke while we rally round to raise the balance needed."

Much later in the evening around six, the TV was on and a man was preaching. Chris decided to listen.

The preaching went on, and then the man said, "The challenge, crisis, trouble ... blindness, the wheelchair ... whatever it is ... will not stop you if you don't let it!"

The wheelchair?! Hmm. Chris paid closer attention.

The man continued. "For you are of God and have overcome. He who is in you is greater than he who is in the world."

Chris knew that the statement was a Bible verse—First John chapter four and verse four. He had quoted it several times.

The man went on. "When you make up your mind to team up with God and His word, and you remain focused and determined to win, no matter the challenges, you will see victory!"

Chris took a deep breath.

"Child of God, don't let the enemy win!"

The man continued and when he began to pray, Chris said Amen.

Stella returned from work shortly after and found Chris' mother alone in the room with Chris.

When the woman shared the idea about the bungalow with Stella, Stella wasn't surprised or upset. With the way her life had been spiralling downward, she didn't expect anything less, and she agreed with the idea. She wouldn't like to live near her parents-in-law; but, under this circumstance, it might not be a bad idea. If she chose to leave Chris later, his family members would be near him.

That night, there was no one to stay in the room with Chris as his mother and wife left around ten.

Chris slept, and when he woke up around two in the morning, he began to think again. He realized that he would have to face the reality that his life had changed ... but there was still a lot he could achieve if he did not give up.

As he decided to find himself again, he knew that it would be a struggle, but he could do it. He had only two choices ... to win this battle or let his circumstance win.

He chose to be the winner. And with that decided, he prayed briefly and slept.

When he woke up later in the morning, he remembered his resolve to win the battle in his life, and he began to speak in tongues. It seemed like such a long time ago since he last spoke in tongues, but he continued for some minutes before he decided to pray in English.

Afterward, he began to think of ways to encourage himself and get his life back.

A voice suddenly told him—*Don't deceive yourself. What can you do? You have nothing left!*

Chris stopped to listen to the words of the voice, and as he considered them, turning them over in his mind, he became discouraged. The voice was right. His life and plans and future and marriage had been taken away from him. *Hmm.*

To pick himself up and move on would be hard, he thought. Could he do it?

"I'm not strong enough, Lord." He told God and began to cry.

When a nurse came in to attend to him, he wiped his tears away and brought his mind back to the day's activities.

He had breakfast and some time later, he was taken away for treatments and therapy. While there, he received a message from his mother that she had arrived and was in his room.

Back in his room much later, a song came to his mind. The song sometimes played on the radio in his car, on his way to work, and he knew only two lines of the lyrics. Whenever the song played, he would move his head to the rhythm, and when it got to the two lines he knew, he would sing along: *Here's a song for all the broken-hearted, I believe you're only getting started.* He never knew he would one day be among the broken-hearted.

Feeling a need to listen to the song now and know the lyrics, he took his phone from his bedside table and went on YouTube to search for it. It didn't take long to find it.

He tapped on the link and as it began to play, he did not move his head or sing along. He listened and looked at the lyrics. He was looking for encouragement or God's voice ... not entertainment.

Are you running 'round in circles with no place to go?
Is there a person in the mirror you don't even know?
Someone still sees who you are, yeah

Were you the kid that was a dreamer, now you don't believe?
Are you the lock that got so broken, now you lost the key?
Someone still loves who you are, yeah.

Chorus:

To anyone who ever lost your way

To everyone who ever felt ashamed

Here's a song for all the broken-hearted

I believe you're only getting started

To anyone who trusts in Jesus' name

Watch your world become forever changed

Here's a song about light from darkness

I believe you're only getting started

... If you only knew the treasure that you really are

If you could understand the measure of the Father's heart

He loves you, He loves you, He loves you

Fall in His arms and let Him wash you clean

He'll tear off the chains so that you can be free

A new life begins and the old is redeemed

Oh, I believe, yeah

Chorus:

To anyone who ever lost your way

To everyone who ever felt ashamed

Here's a song for all the broken-hearted

I believe you're only getting started

To anyone who trusts in Jesus' name

Watch your world become forever changed

Here's a song about light from darkness

I believe you're only getting started.

When the song ended, Chris closed the App and put the phone down.

With a heavy heart, he asked God for the umpteenth time, "What happened, Lord?! What went wrong?" He waited to hear God.

When he heard nothing, he asked God the question again. This time, what came to his mind was a Scripture.

Fear not, for I am with you; Be not dismayed, for I am your God. I will strengthen you, Yes, I will help you, I will uphold you with My righteous right hand.' (Isaiah 41:10 NKJV)

In the evening, he took his phone and opened the Bible App to read God's word. He decided to start reading from John chapter one. However, before he could search for it, a scripture occurred to him. Deciding to read the scripture first, he searched for it— Psalms forty two verse five. He opened the Amplified version and read it:

Why are you in despair, O my soul? And why have you become restless and disturbed within me? Hope in God and wait

expectantly for Him, for I shall again praise Him For the help of His presence.

He read the next verse.

O my God, my soul is in despair within me [the burden more than I can bear]—

He stopped and repeated the words of verse six to God in prayer. He added, "Help me, in Jesus' name."

Then he continued reading the verse six:

Therefore I will [fervently] remember You from the land of the Jordan And the peaks of [Mount] Hermon, from Mount Mizar.

He would have to do that—*fervently remember the Lord*. And he would start right away.

With that decided, he began to speak in tongues. As he did, he began to sense some form of light beyond the darkness in his heart. He believed that God would heal his broken heart even though he didn't know how He would do it.

Chris also resolved to start joining his church's services online. He would start listening to sermons by his pastors and other ministers of God whom he believed in.

When Stella came shortly after and greeted him, he responded briefly. She had not given him an answer, but he hoped she would, soon. He could still sense that she was struggling to hold on, and she might choose to leave him. He resolved to keep to himself so as not to be greatly disappointed.

On Friday morning, he learned that Luke had sent some money to his father for the building of the bungalow. He called Luke and thanked him.

On Monday morning, while he was listening to a sermon about thanksgiving on his phone, he realized that even though he had a long road ahead of him, he still had reasons to be grateful to God.

He began to think of his reasons to be grateful.

One, he was still alive.

Two, he was fortunate to still have full use of his hands and could do some things and take care of himself. Some people were paralysed from the neck down, and couldn't do anything.

Three, he still had his mind intact. What if he could not reason properly anymore?

Four, many people had been very supportive, and they appeared to really care about him.

He began to thank God for the support of families, friends, and the church. Some of them had been visiting him everyday—before and after work, sometimes bringing him food. Some gave him money.

He also thanked God for his boss and colleagues. His boss had said that his full salary would be paid for three months which would terminate at the end of this month of February. The man and some of his colleagues had also made financial donations to support him.

Even the medical personnel and therapists. What would have happened if he did not have these people's support?

He was not sure about Stella's commitment, but she was still with him, and he thanked God for that.

And finally, he thanked God for keeping him alive, for not leaving him even when he tried to stay away from Him, and for the Holy Spirit—his Comforter and Counselor.

He would need to make these people know that he appreciated them, he decided.

Taking a deep breath, he called out to his mother who was in the room with him.

"Yes?" She looked at him. "Do you need something?"

He shook his head and said no.

She waited for him to continue.

"I ... I just want to thank you for your support ... you and Daddy ... for all that you've been doing for me since this problem started in December." He paused, smiled a little, and added, "well maybe I should say since you gave birth to me."

Where is this going, his mother wondered as she blinked back tears. She hoped that he wasn't planning to do something stupid.

"But especially now." He went on. "I appreciate everything."

When he stopped, she asked, "Is there something on your mind that you want to tell me?"

"No, that's it. I just wanted to say thank you."

"I am glad that you're alive." She gave him a watery smile. She added that she and his father and his brothers loved him dearly, and they were praying for him.

Afterward, Chris took his phone, and composed a message on WhatsApp which he began to forward to his phone contacts.

As the nurses, therapists, doctors, and cleaners came into his room to attend to him, he thanked them. And when his brother, other family members, friends, and church members came, he thanked them as well.

Stella arrived in the evening and this time, he responded nicely to her greeting—to her surprise. When he was alone with her, he called her name and thanked her for all that she had been doing for him.

This time, she was the silent one. *Where did that come from?* She wondered.

CHAPTER 9

THAT NIGHT, AS Chris listened to a sermon on healing, miracle, and God's power, he told himself that a miracle was still possible for him. He would put his hope in God.

He also resolved that while he was waiting for his miracle, in spite of the huge setback, he could still live. He would achieve something with his life, even if there was no change in his body.

And even if Stella chose to leave him, he would still live. He would not allow satan to have the last say concerning him.

He continued thinking. What exactly could he do being in a wheelchair? *Hmm.* He would think of something, he resolved.

However, by the time he woke up the next morning, he was feeling hopeless again. How much could he do from the wheelchair? He still had his hands and mind intact, but what could he achieve?

He began to cry again. "What can I do, Lord?"

That day, he didn't pray or read the Bible much.

The next day, a song began to play on the TV station. He didn't quite get the lyrics but he heard a part of it—*Oh, my soul you are not alone. There's a place where fear has to face the God you know.*

Those words ministered to him and when the song ended, he went on YouTube to search for it, so that he could see the lyrics and listen to it again. He found it, and as it began to play on YouTube, he looked at the lyrics.

Oh, my soul,

Oh, how you worry

Oh, how you're weary, from fearing you lost control

This was the one thing, you didn't see coming

And no one would blame you, though, if you cried in private

If you tried to hide it away, so no one knows

No one will see, if you stop believing

Chorus:

Oh, my soul

You are not alone

There's a place where fear has to face the God you know

One more day, He will make a way

Let Him show you how, you can lay this down

'Cause you're not alone

Here and now

You can be honest

I won't try to promise that someday it all works out

'Cause this is the valley

And even now, He is breathing on your dry bones

And there will be dancing

There will be beauty where beauty was ash and stone
This much I know

Chorus

I'm not strong enough, I can't take anymore

(You can lay it down, you can lay it down)

And my shipwrecked faith will never get me to shore

(You can lay it down, you can lay it down)

Can He find me here

Can He keep me from going under

Oh, my soul

You're not alone

There's a place where fear has to face the God you know

One more day, He will make a way

Let Him show you how, you can lay this down

'Cause you're not alone

Oh, my soul, you're not alone...

Chris pondered the words in his heart. *Oh, my soul, you are not alone. There's a place where fear has to face the God you know.*

Yes, he knew God. He was a child of God.

Well, he guessed that it was time for fear to face the God he knew, he resolved.

He remembered his calling. God had not changed His mind about that, he was sure. In bed, he didn't sleep on time as he thought of what steps to take, and the words of the song rang in his ears.

What exactly could he do? And more importantly, what would God want him to do? He prayed and asked God to take control and lead him to what he could do with what was left of him.

After some time, it occurred to him to go online to see what paraplegic people like him did. He did, and came across blogs by men and women with physical challenges. Some of the blogs were irrelevant, while some gave ungodly counsels. He ignored those ones and focused his attention on the good and relevant ones.

As he read the blogs that he selected, he realized that there were a number of things that he could do to help himself. He might not be able to use his legs, and he might depend on people to do certain things, however, he could still use his brain, mouth, hands, and his divine calling. There was no mountain that he and God could not climb together.

One of the writers said that he had been able to do some of the things that doctors told him he would never be able to do again due to physical therapy.

Hmm, he would need to take physical therapy serious, Chris realized.

Another person talked about how changing his diet helped him. And Chris decided that he would change his diet as well; he would cut off foods and drinks that would not help him. He must begin to eat healthy. Changing his diet would be a little difficult, but it could be done. He was willing to do whatever would help him.

While reading the selected blogs, he saw a quote that he liked.

Some things may be too broken to be fixed, but not too broken to be repurposed by God.

He decided to use it as his WhatsApp profile picture. Without delay, he designed a beautiful frame with those words inserted, and with a click, he uploaded the picture to his WhatsApp profile.

When he returned from physical therapy the next day, he took his iPad and began to write down the things that he still possessed which he could put to use. He wrote: *hands; mouth; love; a sound mind; and a divine calling.* Of course, he had the Holy Spirit, and some people who cared about him—friends and family. He intended to put every blessing to use.

God was giving him a purpose and he would not allow satan to take it from him.

He went to bed that night feeling hope rising within him again. He would have to hold on to that hope.

He prayed when he woke up the following morning, and when his therapist came, he told the man that he was ready to do all that was necessary to make him better. He told the man who appeared to be about his age not to spare him, and that whenever he felt lazy, the man should please encourage him to go on.

On the way to the therapy room, he was speaking in tongues. There, he did a lot of physiotherapy. It was tough, but he pushed himself and worked hard. He had to—he didn't have a choice. He must have his life back. He must win this battle!

Back in his room much later, he listened to sermons and Christian songs on TV. And in the night when everywhere was quiet, he talked to God and listened to Him to receive direction.

The next day, he decided to watch some videos of Nick Vujicic on YouTube. The Australian-American evangelist was born without any limbs. However, he did not allow this to limit him as he graduated from a university at the age of twenty one. He eventually got married to a beautiful woman, and they had two sons and two daughters together. Chris also read that Nick was able to type forty three words per minute on a computer.

By the time Chris eventually put his phone down, he was greatly encouraged. If Nick could achieve so much without any limbs, then he was sure that he could achieve a lot with what was left of him.

He prayed, "Lord, use me to Your glory, in Jesus' name." He had finally found the courage to move forward with living his life.

Regularly, Chris went for physiotherapy. There were times when he wanted to give up thinking that the therapy wasn't achieving much. However, the therapists encouraged him, and he continued.

And as he read the Bible daily, prayed, and listened to sermons, he felt closer to God and spiritually stronger.

****

Stella on the other hand, didn't seem to be faring well. On some days, she thought she was coping well; but on other days, she told Jesus, "I can't do this!"

And there were days that she felt too exhausted to pray.

She woke up on the last Saturday of February and remained in bed to pray and think. Chris still expected a response from her. What should it be?

If she asked for divorce, what kind of a Christian would that make her?

But how could she stay? Even Chris had offered her freedom. Should she accept it?

She couldn't make up her mind and she eventually left for the hospital.

The next morning, on Sunday, she went to church. Since the accident, she had not been regularly attending church, and the few times that she did attend, she did not join the choir to minister as usual.

There was a female guest minister that day and at the right time, the minister went to the altar and took the microphone on the glass pulpit. After appreciating the senior pastor and his wife for inviting her to share the word of God with their congregation, she prayed and announced that the sermon topic was *Overcoming the challenges of life.*

"I'll tell you a little about myself." She continued.

Stella listened with rapt attention. Overcoming the challenges of life was a message she needed to hear at this time.

"My husband had an accident that left him paralyzed neck down."

Neck down?! Stella's eyes widened in shock.

"He lost the ability to walk. He could no longer be intimate with me. He could not even hug me. I had to help him to do everything—eat, use the bathroom, the toilet, wear his clothes, get into his wheelchair."

Hmm. *I thank God that Chris can still use his hands and can take care of himself. He can also do certain things around the house. It could have been worse,* Stella realized.

The woman went on. "He could no longer be a provider. We had four children, the oldest was ten and the youngest was two when the accident happened."

Wha-t?!

"That was a very challenging moment in my life and marriage. Waking up and facing the day was very hard for me ... really hard. Someone was employed to take care of him, but even that was not enough because my husband was completely dependent. Even though I was a Christian who loved the Lord, there were moments that I was impatient with him out of frustration. But one day, the

Holy Spirit spoke to my heart and asked me to be calm and patient. He said, 'you can choose to walk away from this problem, but your husband cannot.' My perspective changed from that day."

Hmm, that's true, Stella thought.

"The Holy Spirit also told me that it was okay to ask people for support, and He led me to some very amazing people."

Stella nodded in understanding.

"When there's a challenge, you can either run away, become a victim, or confront it with the help of God. There will be challenges in life, and Jesus Himself said so in the Bible—in the book of John chapter sixteen verse thirty three."

The woman opened her Bible and read it, "These things I have spoken to you, that in Me you may have peace. In the world you will have tribulation; but be of good cheer, I have overcome the world."

She continued. "How you handle the challenges is what matters. And listen ... how you handle them will determine whether or not you overcome them."

As the woman continued preaching, referring to some Scriptures, Stella listened. However, rather than feeling encouraged, she felt troubled. The woman made it seem simple and easy to do, but it wasn't. The woman already had four children when her husband became paralysed. But she did not have any yet. How could she give up her plans? She married the former Chris, not this Chris!

The woman went on. "It wasn't easy but I did my best. My husband eventually died—"

Her husband died? Hmm. Stella stopped to think about it. If Chris died, these challenges would be over, and she would be free to remarry and begin a new life. She would have to think about this later.

On the way home, she thought about it as she had promised herself. Would it not be better for Chris to die than live in a wheelchair for the rest of his life? It might even be God's will for him to die. She wouldn't hurt him, of course. She couldn't—being a Christian. But she could pray about it.

In bed that night, she prayed that if it was God's will for Chris to die, God should take him as soon as possible. That way, Chris would be free of his predicament, and she would be free to move on with her life.

But how would she find another man to marry? she wondered.

Her mind went to Abel. He had visited Chris in the hospital five times, and he sometimes called Stella on phone. He had revealed to her that he was still single and searching for the right woman which surprised her. Not only was he handsome, he also had a nice smile and a soft chuckle that seemed to light up a room. He was a Christian and seemed like a genuinely nice person.

She was becoming quite fond of him, and she wondered if something might be developing between them.

However, as she prayed that Chris would die, her heart condemned her. Somehow, she felt that the prayer was not right, but she told herself that even Chris had said at a time that he wished to die.

The next day, she became bolder and more desperate about the prayer. "God, take Chris away in Jesus' name."

She prayed the prayer for about a week, and then stopped when Chris refused to die. The guilt she felt in her heart did not help matters as well.

She would have to make a decision soon however; she couldn't continue this way.

One night, she decided she would tell Chris the next day that she would like to leave, but by the time she woke up, she was not very sure about the decision again.

In the first week of April, the bungalow was completed with ramps at strategic places. Chris asked for two single beds to be in his room, one for him, and the other for whoever might need to be in the room with him.

"Okay." Stella simply said. The arrangement was okay by her, because she had been wondering how she would sleep on the same bed with him.

She spoke again, "What should I do with our big bed?"

"Give it to whoever needs it." He told her.

"Okay."

They would have to buy a wheelchair for Chris since the one he had been using belonged to the hospital. They decided to get a narrow one that would fit through the doorways in the house.

At home on Saturday, the tenth of April, as Stella packed her clothes and put them in a storage box, she told herself, "Just breathe, Stella, just breathe."

She had to get a grip. She would also need to create time to eat, rest, and take care of herself, she counselled herself.

The twenty-fourth of April, a Saturday, was fixed for moving and that morning, male friends and family members came around and helped Stella move their stuff from their apartment to the new house in record time. Two single beds were put in the master bedroom. A room was arranged for visitors, while their remaining items were stored in the third room.

In the afternoon, some female friends came to clean and arrange the bedrooms and kitchen. One of them brought food, while another brought groceries. They couldn't finish and after church service on Sunday, some of the ladies returned to complete the job.

Her first night in the house, alone in one of the single beds in the master bedroom that she would share with Chris, she decided to write her feelings down.

Lord Jesus, I don't know how to handle this. Won't You help me?! What about children? Love making?

As she wrote them, she cried.

****

On Monday, the twenty-sixth of April, Chris was told that he would be discharged to go home on Friday, the last day of April. Happy, he thanked the doctor. He did a mental calculation and realized that leaving on that day would mean that he spent a month in ICU and four months in this private room.

Stella was in the room with his parents and brother when a nurse came to explain how to take care of him at home. As she talked, Stella realized that being his wife, the responsibility would fall on her, and she took a deep breath.

On the day that Chris was to be discharged, the male nurse came to the hospital and together they went to the house.

In Chris' bedroom, there were two single beds. *Good.* He glanced around and noticed immediately that their framed wedding photograph was on the wall but the black script *'Together Forever'* that was on their bedroom wall in the apartment was missing. He was sad, but he kept quiet.

Some people visited that day and brought food.

Chris would have to go for therapy three times a week—Monday, Wednesday, and Friday. On Monday, he went to therapy in the company of his father and the male nurse, while Stella went to work.

The next day, some friends came to do their laundry and go grocery shopping for them while some others brought food.

If Chris had to go out of the house, the nurse went with him to assist him in getting in and out of places if there was no ramp.

CHAPTER 10

DIFFERENT PEOPLE CALLED Stella to give their opinions on what they thought that she should do about her marriage. Some of them told her what she wanted to hear—that she should leave Chris and move on with her life.

Some others told her to stay.

A few people were not certain about how to handle the situation, and they told her that she was free to do whatever she liked.

Yes, Stella knew that she was free to do whatever she liked. However, as a child of God, she knew that she couldn't do whatever she liked. God's will was important. But what was the will of God? With everything going on, she couldn't think clearly to determine what it was. She was still a Christian, and she would need to spend time in God's presence to hear Him.

She decided to go away on a retreat for some days to think, pray, clear her head, and make a decision.

With her mind made up about the retreat to be alone with God, she decided to inform one of Chris' very close friends first.

He understood and said that she should go if it would help her. He added, "I must commend you ... you've been strong. Things have changed and that can be hard to accept. You have to decide on what's best for you."

Afterward, she informed Chris' parents and brother, and then Chris. He simply said okay.

While she was looking for some pictures in her e-mail the next day, she stumbled on their wedding pictures. She stopped and took a long look at them. As she looked at Chris in the pictures, she realized that the same Chris still lived in the broken body. He was her husband. How could she leave him? But how could she stay? She closed the pictures with the plan to look at them during her retreat.

The next thing would be to decide where to go for the retreat. She would have loved to go to *Divine Rest Guest House* where they had their honeymoon as she really liked the place. The beautiful Guest House was owned by a Christian, and was established to meet the needs of Christians for retreats and events. It had large rooms and suites, and there were security men at its two gates.

However, she wouldn't go there because it held too many beautiful memories for her. Besides, she wasn't sure that she'd be able to afford to spend so much at this time. It might be better to look for a cheap but decent guest house.

She asked some friends and one of them recommended a place that was decent in her opinion. It was not far from Stella's office, and she chose to go on Thursday, the twenty-seventh of May, since Friday and Monday were public holidays. She would return home on Monday.

That Thursday, she packed a travelling bag and put it in the boot of her car when she was leaving the house in the morning. When she closed at work in the evening, she drove to the place.

There, she paid for a room with an attached bathroom, and a male attendant asked her to follow him. When they reached a door, he unlocked it with a key, and turned a light on. As Stella stepped inside, she glanced around. The room was indeed decent, but rather small. It had a single bed, a table, a plastic chair, a closet, and an air conditioner. She walked over to the bathroom door, opened it, and peered inside. There were some stains on the walls, but the shower and the toilet seat were clean. She closed the door.

She asked the attendant about how she would order food from the kitchen. He answered her questions and left.

Stella locked her door, placed an order for food, and while she waited for it to be delivered, she unpacked her bag. Soon, her food was delivered and she ate. Afterward, she showered, and in bed, she prayed briefly, asking God to talk to her during this retreat. Then she slept.

At about three-thirty in the morning, she woke up and began to think. Everything about her life had been planned out by her, but nothing was the same anymore. She prayed for some time and then stopped to listen for God's voice.

One of the questions that had been plaguing her mind resurfaced: If what happened to Chris had happened to her, would he stay with her or leave?

As she thought about it, she could hear the Holy Spirit telling her that her decision should not be based on what Chris might do, but on the word of God.

She carried her Bible to read. She opened it and found that it opened to Proverbs chapter three. She decided to read it and began from verse one. When she got to verses five and six, she paused as she felt a stirring of her spirit.

Trust in the LORD with all your heart,
And lean not on your own understanding;
In all your ways acknowledge Him,
And He shall direct your paths.

As she meditated on the verses and their meanings, she felt God talking to her, to deal with her plans, concerns, and questions.

Another thing occurred to her … if she was feeling this way, then Chris must be feeling worse. He was very active and full of life … not the kind to sit in one place for long. It must be devastating for him to lose his legs and independence. She realized that she was supposed to encourage him; help him to pull through, and not add to his challenges, if she truly loved him.

She eventually slept back and woke up around nine on Friday morning. After taking her bath, she returned to bed and, while praying and speaking in tongues, she remembered their wedding pictures that she saw in her e-mail. Still speaking in tongues, she took her phone and opened her e-mail. She went to the wedding pictures and stared at some of them for some minutes.

Their wedding program was also in the e-mail and she clicked on it. She started looking at it from page one and when she got to page three, she began to read the words out.

"Dearly beloved, we are gathered here in the sight of God and in the presence of these witnesses, to join together this man and this woman in holy matrimony; which is an honourable estate, instituted of God. It is therefore not to be entered into unadvisedly, but reverently, discreetly, and in the fear of God."

She put the phone down beside her and took a deep breath as she remembered the ceremony.

She also remembered that the pastor charged them in his sermon to be firm in their commitment to one another.

He had added, "Be united and undivided. As you seek to know God's will and obey it, whatever it is, you will find peace and joy."

Her mind came back to the issue at hand. If she left her husband, she would not be the first wife to do such a thing. Chris was expecting her to leave, and his parents had told her at a time to do whatever she thought was best for her.

However, as she thought and prayed more, and considered leaving Chris to start afresh, she did not have peace in her heart.

She had said "I do" on their wedding day. Should she say "I don't" now because of his paralysis?

On Saturday, she was still praying when another question occurred to her. She had loved him deeply. Was her love based on who or what he was? Did she love him because he was handsome and could walk?

She thought about it and told herself—no. She loved him because of who he was as a person. Besides, she prayed and she believed that she heard God tell her to go ahead.

Hmm, she would have to honour God, she thought.

It will not be easy! Her heart screamed at her.

As she gave this fear a thought, she remembered that a Scripture said something about trials. Taking her phone, she searched for it, and read it.

Consider it pure joy, my brothers, whenever you face trials of many kinds, because you know that the testing of your faith develops perseverance. Perseverance must finish its work so that you may be mature and complete not lacking anything. Blessed is the man who perseveres under trial, because when he has stood the test, he will receive the crown of life that God has promised to those who love him.

She shook her head sadly as she thought about the implications of saying yes to what she believed God was telling her to do.

Can I do it? Yes, she told herself. She could do it even though it would not be easy. She had a long road ahead, but she would have to trust God.

What would the people who encouraged her to leave say when they learned of her decision? One of them in particular—a woman—might think that she was stupid.

She considered this and told herself that God's opinion was more important than the woman's. If God was pleased with her, then she would be satisfied, she told herself.

As she continued praying and reading the word of God, she realized that she should not leave Chris because of her own desires.

"But do I still love him?" She asked herself aloud. After a moment of careful consideration, she got her answer—she wasn't sure of what she felt for him at the moment due to everything that had been happening, but she still cared for him.

She would stay in her marriage.

With that decided, she began to cry. "Lord, I give You full control. I give this to You!"

She also surrendered all the plans that she had made, and her hopes, to God. She would have to trust that God knew what He was doing. He would not abandon her and everything would be alright eventually.

On Sunday morning, she joined her church's service online and as she listened to the sermon, she was convinced that she had made the right decision.

Later in the evening, she called her pastor, told him that she was on a retreat, and had decided to stand by her husband.

"Hmm, that's good. Have you communicated that to him?" He wanted to know.

"No sir. I'm still at the retreat centre. I'll be going back home tomorrow."

"Ok. I believe that you have made the right decision, but i need to point something out."

Stella listened.

"The Bible talks about counting the cost. Doing that will help a person to be well prepared. Do you understand?"

"Yes sir."

"In this matter ... you need to count the cost, and I'll break it down for you. Are you listening to me?"

"Yes sir."

"As his wife, you have an obligation to show him love. And so, if you choose to stay, you will have to show him love. You will need to compliment him, say nice things, and encourage him. Whatever you think that you need to do as his wife. Don't stay and take care of him with resentment or grudgingly. You must not make him feel like he's a liability. Have you thought about these things, and are you ready to do them?"

"Yes sir. I think that I have." She answered. "I don't know what lies ahead, but I've decided to honour God and I know that He will help me."

"Good. I'm happy to hear that." The pastor said.

He prayed for her and promised to visit her family soon.

After the call, Stella sent a message to Chris to inform him that she would return home the next day. She sent another one to ask how he was doing. He simply said, *I'm fine. Okay.*

As she read his reply, she decided that they would need to have a long talk. His attitude toward her would have to change.

On the way home the next day, which was the last day of May, she was still thinking. She didn't feel that she would ever forget the day Chris had the accident and the call that changed everything she had planned. But she now had her peace.

She stopped at a store to buy the cucumber and pawpaw that Chris liked.

At home, Chris was in the living room with his parents, and she greeted them. She went to the bedroom she shared with Chris and some minutes after, she emerged in at-home clothes. In the kitchen, she cut the pawpaw and brought the small slices in bowls. She served Chris and his parents before sitting down to eat hers.

Much later in their bedroom, Chris was the first to talk. "So, what's your decision?"

She took a deep breath before she said, "We are married. I'm your wife."

"So?"

"We're in this together. God will help us."

"I don't know what that means. Are you staying with me or not?"

"I'm with you, I'm not going anywhere."

He was happy to hear that, but his face did not show the emotion as he asked her, "Are you sure about this? You don't have to stay with me, you know."

She frowned and stared at him. That was not what he was supposed to say. "Are you trying to push me away, Chris?!"

He wanted to say ... *no, I'm not. I'm only trying to make you know that you can leave.*

But he changed his mind, returned the stare and said, "Maybe I am."

Surprised, she paused as if to absorb this, and then she retorted, "Oh, really? Why, if I may ask?"

"It's because I know some wives who chose to leave their paraplegic husbands."

She was quiet for some seconds as she tried to understand what he was driving at. "So?"

"And because there's not much left to offer you." He added and looked away.

Understanding dawned on her. She got up from her bed and came to sit on his bed. Putting a hand on his shoulder, she told him, "I'm sorry that this happened to you. As I said, we're in it together."

"My legs are broken."

"If your legs are broken, then we're broken together ... because we are one."

She reached for his hand and as they talked, both of them wept.

Then he thanked her for choosing to stay. He also made her know that he had been talking to God and he believed that God would make him walk again one day.

They discussed and decided to consult with specialists about the issues of sexual intimacy, child adoption, and IVF.

They also decided that her bed would be brought beside his so they could sleep together. They eventually prayed and slept.

The next day, Stella and the nurse moved her bed to join Chris'. Much later in their room, Chris told her that he had decided to rejoin the workforce, and had started applying to places for a job he could do from home.

"I'd also like to start attending church physically." He could still teach in church.

They talked about it and decided to discuss with the senior pastor.

CHAPTER 11

WHEN THE PASTOR visited Chris and Stella on Friday evening, he was glad to know that Chris was ready to attend church in person and resume Sunday morning Bible Study teaching.

Afterward, he began to counsel Chris concerning his marriage. "You may not be able to walk yet, but I'm sure you can show love. Am I right?"

Chris laughed. "Yes sir."

"Good, you should show love to your wife. Don't focus solely on yourself."

Yes, he could show love, Chris thought. And he still loved his wife. Besides, God had already spoken to him about it. He was just sad that he could no longer be a normal husband and would not be able to do some of the things that he once did with and for Stella.

It was as if the pastor read his mind as he said, "You may not be able to do some things you did in the past. However, you can talk to her, be an excellent listener, and whatever else you can do. Just as she has to make sure that your needs are being met, you need to make sure that her needs are being met too, as much as you can."

"Yes sir." Chris responded, and then moved his wheelchair to Stella's side, held her hand, and looked at the pastor.

The pastor smiled in approval at the show of affection and added, "In a situation like this, communication will greatly help."

Chris nodded. "Yes sir."

The pastor advised Stella to create time to rest. Afterward, he prayed for them, and left.

****

In the afternoon of the next day, Chris' brother in Canada called Stella and said that Chris asked him to thank her on his behalf.

Surprised, she chuckled and said, "I'm simply doing what I'm supposed to do. He's my husband."

About an hour after, while Stella was folding her clothes in the bedroom, one of Chris' friends called her and said the same thing—Chris wanted him to thank Stella on his behalf. Stella smiled.

It occurred to her to appreciate the people who had supported her family one way or the other since Chris had the accident. As soon as she finished folding the clothes, she sat down, composed a message, and sent it to them.

The following week, Stella called a fertility specialist, fixed an appointment to come in on Friday, the eleventh of June, and on that day, she and Chris went there. The specialist, a woman, answered their questions about their options to have a baby.

She also counselled them on how to handle sexual intimacy. She told Stella, "Let him know what you need him to do." And looking at Chris, she said, "Tell your wife what you like."

The woman added, "It may be awkward initially but it will get better with time. Simply focus on your love and on pleasing one another."

On Saturday, while discussing, Chris revealed to Stella some of his plans to get his life back on course. He would like to create a YouTube channel for what he had in mind, and when he showed her some things he had been writing and recording, she liked them. He said that he was already talking to some of his friends about the plan.

He would need an opening song for the YouTube channel, and he asked her to record a song with him.

"I found the song on YouTube, however, I need just the first part of it." He said and then sang it.

She liked the song and agreed to learn it. In bed later, she went on YouTube, searched for the song, and considered the lyrics.

Fear, you don't own me
There ain't no room in this story
And I ain't got time for you
Telling me what I'm not
Like you know me,
Well guess what?
I know who I am
I know I'm strong

And I am free
Got my own identity
So fear, you will never be welcome here.

She and Chris began to practice the song together.

****

On the first Saturday of July, one of Chris' friends came to the house, and the song was recorded.

The friend came a week after to record Chris' first podcast video. In it, Chris introduced himself and said a little about his physical challenge.

The video didn't take more than an hour. The friend said that he would need to edit the video and would send it to Chris within a couple of days.

While Chris waited for the video, he opened the YouTube channel that he named *Life & Living with Chris*. On it, he planned to discuss different issues ranging from faith in God, life, love, and marriage ... to how to handle challenges including disabilities. He would also reveal his daily life in a wheelchair and how he and his wife were coping, in order to inspire people to trust God and appreciate the gift of life.

When the edited video was sent to him on Wednesday, he uploaded it on the YouTube channel and shared the link with his families and friends. Stella did the same.

In his second video, which was recorded on Saturday, the twenty-fourth of July, Chris said more about the accident, how he had wanted to commit suicide when he learned that he might never walk again, and how God had brought him back from the brink of disaster.

The video was edited, and Chris uploaded it on Thursday.

On Sunday, the first of August, Stella got the invitation for Lekan's wedding. It would hold on the first Saturday of September in Lekan's church, and she decided she would attend. She had not attended any social event since Chris' accident in December. Besides, Lekan had been there for her since the accident. She told Chris about the wedding, and he encouraged her to attend.

Two days after, on Tuesday, Chris received an e-mail from one of the companies that he had applied to. It was an international company based in the USA, and he would be having a job interview on phone on Friday afternoon. If he got the job, he would work online, and get paid in US dollars. He told Stella about it and they prayed that he would get it.

On the day, the interview started promptly and lasted about an hour. He didn't think that it went well and that made him feel a little discouraged. However, to his greatest surprise, he learned on Wednesday that he got the job and would be expected to start in three weeks' time, on the first of September.

****

On Saturday, the fourth of September, Stella left the house for Lekan's wedding. As she sat in the church and looked at Lekan and her groom, Victor, Stella couldn't help remembering Lola's wedding. She had attended with Chris. And she would have attended Lekan's wedding with Chris if he hadn't been confined to a wheelchair.

Her mind was brought back to the present when Lekan was handed a microphone, and she announced that she had a song to sing to her husband, Victor—*I see Jesus in your eyes*.

Stella knew the song, and as Lekan sang it, she sang along quietly.

At the wedding reception, a female gospel singer in Lekan's church was on standby with her band to sing, and when the newly wedded couple was ready to enter the hall, she began to sing *E se gan ni* by Chigozie Wisdom.

Stella joined Mercy and some of Lekan's friends, and as Lekan and Victor danced in, they followed them, dancing.

****

The eighteenth of September was Chris' thirty-first birthday, and casually dressed, he and Stella went to a restaurant in their neighborhood for lunch where she gave him a gift. His nurse was with them, and he used Chris' camera to take pictures and also capture the moment on video.

As they ate chicken and chips, he asked her if she had any plan for her own birthday, which was about a month away—the twelfth of October.

When she said no, he suggested going to a particular restaurant for dinner.

Knowing that the restaurant was not cheap, she shook her head. "Thank you, but we don't have to. Let's save our money for other important things."

He chuckled and dismissed her excuse. "It won't cost much. Besides, this is for your birthday."

"I know, but it's not necessary."

He eventually got her to agree to the idea and to also take the day off work.

The next day, Chris reviewed the video that his nurse recorded and the pictures taken. He edited them and uploaded them on his YouTube channel.

A week after, Stella did a video with him in which she talked about herself and how she had felt discouraged when she learned that Chris would not be able to walk again. The video was to encourage spouses of paraplegics.

Chris also started a blog.

As he continued writing and talking in videos about his experiences, family life, faith, and how God had been helping him and his wife, he realized that they were helping him to heal emotionally.

Doing these things also gave him fulfilment. He was glad that he had some things to do, and people were watching the videos and reading the stories he had to share.

When it occurred to him to turn his story into a book, he shared the idea with Stella, and soon, began to work on it.

****

On Stella's birthday, Chris prayed for her when she woke up. At about six in the evening, they left the house with his nurse who got behind the wheel of Stella's car, while Stella and Chris sat on the backseat and held hands.

As Stella looked out the window on her side, she was lost in thought. She was grateful to God for His faithfulness. She had thought that all hope was lost for her and Chris. She had not been able to sense the presence of God when she realized that Chris might never walk again but God was there all the time.

She had also thought that she had lost the man she married, but God had preserved him. God had also worked in Chris and now, he seemed a better man and a better Christian.

Chris had also become a better listener. If she had something to say, he would give her his full attention and advise her. And because he didn't go out much, they were able to spend more time together, and she enjoyed being with him.

Chris was a fighter, and she was learning some things from him. She wondered if she would have been able to bounce back as he had done if what happened to him had happened to her.

There were days that he seemed upset and a little discouraged, but he tried to quickly overcome the feeling. One of the situations that usually upset him was if he needed something but had to wait until he got help, and sometimes the help did not come on time. But he tried to do things himself, and would ask Stella for assistance only if he couldn't do the thing. And if it was something she couldn't do, he would call his brother or a friend to assist.

He thanked her whenever she helped him. He also thanked her for cooking and performing household duties—which he didn't do before the accident.

He also asked people to help him get gifts to surprise her. People no longer called her to thank her on behalf of Chris because she had told Chris to stop asking people to call her. It embarrassed her. Besides, there was no need for that. She could see that he appreciated all that she did, and that was enough for her, after all, she was his wife.

She still loved him, and she could say that their love had become stronger.

She thanked God for not giving up on her when she wanted to give up—when she felt overwhelmed and lost. She thanked God for gently leading her back to His path for her. She was glad that she did not leave Chris.

She was also glad that God did not answer her prayer to make Chris die. That was a foolish and selfish prayer, she now realized.

She had also thought that they would struggle financially because of expenses, and probably depend on the generosity of some people. However, God had made a way for them. Chris now had a job that paid almost triple of his salary before the accident—without having to go out! And aside teaching a Bible study class in church, he was also a Christian YouTuber, a blogger, and an aspiring author.

You are an amazing God, she mouthed.

They eventually arrived at the restaurant. The nurse parked the car where there was a ramp for Chris' wheelchair, and they alighted. The nurse took Chris' camera and began to record as Stella walked beside Chris.

At the door of the restaurant, Stella stepped back and waited for Chris to enter first, but he asked her to enter.

"Today is about you." He said with a smile teasing the edges of his mouth.

She came to the front and opened the door.

"Happy Birthday!"

What?! Her eyes revealed her surprise as she looked at the faces of the people before her—Chris' and her family members, Mercy and her husband, Lekan and her husband, Lola and her husband, and some other friends.

Chris saw her face break into a beautiful smile, and that made him happy. He loved to see her smile.

Stella greeted everyone, and then turned to Chris. "How did you plan this and I didn't know?"

Everyone laughed.

"Thank you." She bent down and kissed him.

They all went to a reserved area where they sat down to eat and celebrate Stella. Chris and some of the others gave her gifts.

When they finished and got ready to leave, Stella got behind Chris and began to push his wheelchair. *We are broken together,* she thought with a smile.

Chris was also smiling. He had another surprise in store for Stella in December. He had arranged for a middle-aged woman to come to the house to stay for three days, from the twenty-fourth to the twenty-sixth of December, to cook and take care of the house while Stella relaxed and did whatever she would like to do. This would be one of his Christmas gifts to her, to make up for last year's Christmas when she slept on the floor of a hospital room.

Much later in bed at home, Chris turned the bedroom light off, and then put his left hand down. Stella snuggled close, put her head on his shoulder and her left hand on his chest.

As he put his right hand on her waist, he asked her, "Hope you enjoyed your birthday."

"Yes, I did. Thank you so much. I love you." She said in almost a whisper.

"I love you, baby." He responded and kissed the top of her head.

ALSO BY TAIWO IREDELE ODUBIYI

Fiction

Pratt Sisters Series
In Love for Us * Tears on My Pillow * To Love Again

Femi and Ibie Series
With This Ring * The Forever Kind of Love

Agape Campus Church Series
You Found Me * Life Goes On * My Desire

Bible Stories
What Changed You? * Too Much of a Good Thing

The Past Series
Shadows from the Past * This Time Around * Then Came You

Baby Miracle Series
Oh Baby! * Sea of Regrets

Redirected Series
Is it Me You're Looking for? * Marriage on Fire
* Shipwrecked With You * Christmas to Remember * She Who
Has a Man * Comfort and Joy

Mercy & friends Series
The Forever Kind of Love * If You Could See Me Now
* Accidentally Yours

Stand Alone Titles
Love Fever * Love on the Pulpit * My First Love * The One for
Me * When A Man Loves a Woman   * I'll Take You There *
Never Say Never!

For Children
Rescued by Victor * No One is a Nobody
* Greater Tomorrow * The Boy Who Stole
* Joe and His Stepmother, Bibi * Nike & the Stranger
* Billy the Bully * Jonah's First Day of School
* Bimbo Learns a Lesson

Nonfiction
30 Things Husbands Do That Hurt Their Wives
* 30 Things Wives Do That Hurt Their Husbands
* Rape & How to Handle it * Devotionals for Singles
* God's Words to Singles * God's Words to Couples
* God's Words to Older Adults
* Real Answers, Real Quick! (for singles)
* Real Answers, Real Quick! (for couples)
* Divine Instructions to live by – 1
* Divine Instructions to live by – 2
* God's Words to Women in Ministry

ABOUT THE AUTHOR

Taiwo Iredele Odubiyi is a Pastor and the Executive President of TenderHearts Family Support Initiative, a Non-Governmental Organization, and Pastor Taiwo Odubiyi Ministries. She has a deep and strong passion for relationships and expresses this in ministries—nationally and internationally—to children, teenagers, singles, women and couples. She reaches out to these groups through counseling, seminars and programs such as Tenderheartslink, an online program for Christian singles and couples. Married and blessed with children, she is the host of the YouTube program—It's all about you!

This is the thirty-first of her soul-lifting and life-changing novels.

I love hearing from the readers of my books. If this book has blessed you, please send your comments to:

WhatsApp: +1(443)694-6228

Website: www.pastortaiwoodubiyi.org

Facebook: Pastor Mrs. Taiwo Odubiyi

Pastor Taiwo Iredele Odubiyi's novels & books

Twitter: @pastortaiwoodub

Instagram: @pastortaiwoiredeleodubiyi

If you have friends and loved ones, then you do have people you should bless with copies of these very interesting and life-changing novels and books!